KILLER CAST & DEADLY SPLASH

A CRUISE SHIP COZY MYSTERY SERIES BOOK 3

MEL MCCOY

Copyright © 2020 by Mel McCoy

All rights reserved.

No part of this book may be reproduced in any form or by any electronic or mechanical means, including information storage and retrieval systems, without written permission from the author, except for the use of brief quotations in a book review.

This is a work of fiction. Names, places, characters, and incidents are either the product of the author's imagination or are used fictitiously, and any resemblance to any actual persons, living or dead, organizations, events or locales is entirely coincidental.

CHAPTER 1

Ruth Shores struggled to keep her head up. She took another sip of her coffee as her friend, Loretta Moran, punched a key on the computer, and then another. She was slow, but deliberate. Loretta lifted her head from the keyboard and looked at the screen while grabbing the mouse, clicking on an image. The tiny picture grew in size, taking up the entire fifteen-inch screen.

"There he is. Rafael Javiera," Loretta said, leaning back in her chair. "Tall, dark, and handsome himself."

Ruth craned her neck to get a better look at the photo her friend had pulled up on the computer screen. They were in the Orca Internet Cafe, where Loretta had been rambling on about a telenovela show called *Darkness into Light* and how the cast and crew would be aboard the ship for the latest excursion. Her best friend's excitement couldn't be contained, and so the best thing Ruth could do for the time being was to humor her, but truthfully, she wasn't a fan of over-dramatized television. She'd rather read a good G-rated romance novel or mystery.

"He plays Romeo in the show. Isn't he gorgeous?" Loretta asked, staring at the screen, her eyes drifting into a dream-like state. Ruth had to admit that the man was a very good-looking guy. The typical soap opera star. An ideal Latin lover with whom these shows liked to tempt their viewers. He had dark eyes and long, black lashes, and one of the brightest smiles she'd ever seen.

"He's a little young for you, don't you think?" Ruth said with a grin.

Her friend swatted her hand playfully. "That's not the point."

"There's a point?"

"Haven't you been listening? I heard the four biggest stars from the show are going to be on the ship to shoot the season finale on Mermaid's Cay! Rumor has it, this season is going to have a huge twist." Loretta cupped her face in excitement. "I just can't believe it! I'll be serving Romeo himself!"

"Isn't that the dream—to serve the rich and beautiful."

"You don't get it. Anyway, Rafael accepted my request, and we're now friends."

"I don't think he's really your friend. That's probably just one of his employees on his account—he's got better things to do than sit on a computer."

"Ha! Shows what you know," Loretta said. "He doesn't use a computer. He uses his cell phone. In fact, he has it with him all the time, and between takes, he checks his accounts. I hate to say this Ruth, but you need to get with the times."

Her friend was right. Ruth really didn't know how all the internet stuff worked, even though her granddaughters, Emma and Sarah, seemed to be on it every waking hour. She'd just assumed that the rich and famous were too busy to keep up with social media every day.

"Of course," Loretta continued, combing her fingers through her permed blonde hair, fluffing it a bit. "I know that because he invited me into a group thing. It has behind-the-scenes and interviews where he talks to everyone about his day-to-day. I think it's exclusive too. You have to be invited."

Ruth shook her head.

"Here, let me show you." Loretta clicked on a video. On-screen, Romeo was in a big, white room with modern paintings, a grand piano behind him, and a bar. There were several people standing behind him—two men and two women. The men, including Romeo, were wearing tuxedos, and the two women wore beautiful gowns and dangling earrings that glittered in the lights.

"Romeo here. My friends, we have just won the telenovela Telly Award!" He held up a trophy that looked much like an Emmy, only the gold figurine had pointed wings and was standing on a solid, black marble platform. Everyone in the video began hooting and clinking champagne glasses in celebration. "Can you believe it?" he continued and looked at his friends behind him, making a show of feeling the weight of the trophy. "I can't believe how heavy it is."

One of the men in a tuxedo grabbed the Telly Award from Romeo. "Don't finger it up." The man looked at the trophy with a sparkle in his eyes. "This will forever be my pride and joy." He placed it on a shelf on the wall behind the piano. Everyone in the room applauded.

Romeo looked back into the camera. "My friends, that is our producer, Jay Juan. Isn't he fantastic?" He paused a moment, as if waiting for a response, then continued, "We couldn't have done this without him. He's a true winner and will be the holder of our award. But he said we can come visit it whenever we want."

Someone in the background shouted, "You just can't touch it!"

Romeo let out a chuckle. "Okay, my friends, I will

now celebrate with my colleagues." Salsa music started up, and one of the beautiful women called out to him. Romeo looked behind him, putting a finger up to say to give him one minute. He turned back to the camera. "I must go now. Thank you for watching!"

The video froze.

"Isn't that wonderful?" Loretta asked, a smile spread across her light fuchsia-painted lips. "That's when they won the Telly Award for best telenovela show last year. It's my favorite video on here. Mostly, he just talks about his day-to-day life. You know, you should really set up an account. I could help you."

"No, thank you. One of my granddaughters tried to set me up with that Photobook thing, but I couldn't figure the darn thing out."

Loretta shook her head. "It's called Friendbook."

"Oh, right. Friendbook. Anyway, it's just too confusing. So much beeping and things popping up and changing color. Even after I closed it, it kept chiming." Ruth rubbed her head as if she had a headache just thinking about it. "It's just not for me."

Loretta chuckled. "You can't just close out of it. You have to sign out. And those chimes you hear, they're called notifications."

"Yeah. My granddaughter, Emma, said something like that, but I gave up and told her to get me off of it."

Just then, Ruth felt a presence quickly emerge from behind her.

"There you two are," came a familiar voice.

Ruth and Loretta spun around to see the ship's kitchen manager and their boss, Janice Hassley, standing behind them, her arms crossed and her usually perfect, tight bun disarrayed. She looked frazzled. "Break time's over."

Ruth looked at her watch. "We still have at least ten minutes."

Janice shook her head. "We're having a cupcake crisis in the kitchen."

Ruth furrowed her eyebrows. "Crisis?"

"John mixed the cream cheese frosting in with the marshmallow whip or something." Janice put the palm of her hand to her forehead. "It's a complete disaster in there. We need two new batches of frosting, and all of those hundreds of cupcakes need to be decorated. The guests will be boarding in only a couple of hours, and all I have for them are naked cakes."

Loretta's brow furrowed. "How did he mix that up?"

Janice let out a frustrated breath. "Oh, I don't know. Just hurry up. I have dinner prep to worry about right now."

CHAPTER 2

Ruth burst through the kitchen doors, Loretta tailing her. John glanced up with his signature deer-in-headlights look. As Janice had said, there were hundreds of cupcakes covering every inch of the kitchen. There wasn't a bare counter or table in sight. Immediately, John tried to explain, but he was talking so fast it wasn't coherent enough for Ruth to comprehend.

Ruth put her hand up and John stopped talking.

"Slow down, John." Ruth looked around, assessing the situation. Among the many cupcakes was a small counter space where mixing was done. There were several mixing bowls, three of which were dripping with a white liquid. The other bakers at their own stations were also quiet and seemed to have slowed down, probably to see how this show would play out.

Turning her gaze back to John, Ruth said, "Loretta and I were only gone for fifteen minutes. All you were supposed to do was make several batches of the marshmallow whip. What happened?"

"That's what I was doing," John said, "but I ran out of the larger bowls for the mixer, so I had to use the smaller ones, and I was transferring the frosting into the larger bowl. I must have dumped the marshmallow whip into the cream cheese."

Ruth closed her eyes and rubbed her temple. "Okay, here's what we are going to do. John, I want you to start a new batch of cream cheese frosting, and I will redo the marshmallow whip." Ruth turned to Loretta. "You stick to your original duties."

"The strawberry shortcake cupcakes?" Loretta asked.

"Right."

Loretta gave a curt nod. "I'm on it."

The three of them dispersed, going their separate ways, pulling ingredients and measuring. Ruth had gotten everything she needed for the marshmallow whip and was ready to begin the whipping process, when she decided to check on John.

Ruth walked over to him as he was pouring milk into

the mixing bowl. "Did you double check the ingredients?" she asked.

"Sure did, boss."

Ruth sighed. "I'm not your boss."

"I know, but it sounds better than supervisor or mentor."

Ruth couldn't help but smile at his response. The young twenty-two-year-old man might've been a mess who created havoc in the kitchen, but he certainly knew how to charm a person. He had a kind soul, and most importantly, he had heart. He was also learning very quickly how to bounce back from a mistake or complete disaster, which was most important for keeping your head above water in the kitchen, especially aboard the *Splendor of the Seas* and under the management of Janice Hassley.

"All right, then." Ruth put up a finger. "Fire up the mixer, John!"

John smiled, his fine creases framing his blue eyes. He flipped the switch on the mixer, and immediately, Ruth could sense that something wasn't quite right. But before her brain could fully form what that problem was, a storm of liquid and cream cheese showered them incessantly with a milky goo. It took a while for Ruth's mind to catch up to what was happening as she was bombarded with more and more of the white goop.

"Turn it off, John! Turn it off!"

Frantically, John turned off the mixer, and they both stood dumbfounded and quiet, looking at each other. They were both completely covered in a layer of milk, egg, and heavy cream.

Finally, Ruth wiped a splatter of cream cheese from just below her eye with a finger. "John, I think you forgot to set the mixer to a lower speed."

"Uh, right."

Loretta let out a snort before fully committing to a whole-hearted belly laugh. Before Ruth knew it, the rest of the baking staff was doubling over in a fit of laughter.

Grabbing a towel, Ruth dabbed the rest of the cream cheese mixture off her face. "Laugh it up, everyone."

Loretta walked over. "I'm sorry, but you literally have egg on your face." She put a hand up to her mouth, as if she were trying to stifle another explosive laugh.

The rest of the morning and into the afternoon, the baking staff was frantic, decorating cakes and arranging them for presentation for the new wave of passengers. On top of that, there was much excitement surrounding the stars of the popular telenovela show being aboard the ship and shooting the season finale episode on one of the islands. It seemed like all of the staff knew about the show, and there was much chatter about it, but it didn't seem to slow them down.

Ruth had to pull a couple of the bakers from their stations to help with the cupcakes. She was all too aware that it had been the second time she'd left John alone during pre-boarding prep, and it was the second time he had caused calamity in the kitchen. Ruth had to make sure it was the last, deciding not to leave John alone next time.

In the banquet hall, Ruth stood next to Loretta as they watched the passengers gather into the large room, chatting and eating or retrieving food from the massive yet beautiful dessert display that Ruth and her staff had worked on tirelessly that day. From the corner of her eye, Ruth saw Janice shaking the hands of various people and talking. She was smiling, and Ruth let out a sigh of relief. They had pulled it off, again.

"Another crisis adverted," Loretta said. "Sometimes, I don't know how we do it."

"Me neither."

"Oh, no. Here comes Janice." Loretta straightened herself and smoothed out the front of her uniform.

"Ruth," Janice said, quickly approaching. "Mrs. Wenchester is on board again. You know what that means."

Ruth let out a light groan. Mrs. Wenchester was a rich, grouchy old woman who was a regular passenger on the ship. She was basically a hermit with her five-pound Yorkshire terrier, Isabella. They rarely came out of their suite, which would be fine by Ruth and the rest of the staff, only that she had to have her food—and just about everything else—delivered to her. Though, she couldn't blame Mrs. Wenchester for never wanting to leave her suite. It was enormous and beautiful. But the woman was also unbearable to be around, even if it was only for a few minutes.

"I need someone to deliver Mrs. Wenchester's evening snack," Janice said.

"She still wants a slice of Boston Cream pie?" Ruth asked.

"No, this time she wants a fresh eclair every night at exactly 9 p.m. I know it's after your shift, but I don't have anyone else that can do it tonight. Can you do that for me? Just this one time, I promise."

Ruth nodded. What choice did she have? "Of course, Janice."

Janice flashed her a big smile. "Great!" She turned on her heels and began to walk away, but then she turned and called out, "Oh, and don't be late. You know how she gets if you're late."

"Don't worry, I've got it," Ruth said as Janice disappeared in the crowd.

Loretta looked at Ruth. "Better you than me."

Before Ruth could respond, there was a hand on her shoulder. The heavy scent of white musk and Aqua Net hairspray dominated her nostrils. "Hey, you two." It was Wanda, one of the women from "the gang" that Loretta liked to spend time with on the ship, playing the slot machines in the casino and drinking martinis. Wanda was short like Ruth, but a little rounder in the midsection. Her poofy red hair looked much darker in the dimly lit banquet room, which made her round face seem paler than usual. That, or it was her extra-dark maroon lipstick she'd been experimenting with lately, in a failed attempt to make her thin lips look fuller. "Did you know that the stars from *Darkness into Light* are aboard?"

Loretta gasped, turning around. "I know! Everyone is talking about it."

"Ruth, aren't you excited?" Wanda asked.

"She doesn't watch it," Loretta chimed in.

It was Wanda's turn to gasp. "No! You haven't seen the show?"

Ruth shook her head. "I just never got into the soap opera thing."

Wanda arched an eyebrow. "Never got into the soap opera *thing?*" She turned to Loretta. "You hear this?"

Loretta shrugged.

"So, you haven't seen the show?" Wanda continued. "Now I've heard it all. That should be a crime."

"I tried telling her that," Loretta said.

Ruth didn't doubt that Loretta probably had. But regardless, Loretta and Wanda were very much alike. The only difference Ruth could discern was that Loretta was taller and that Wanda preferred bolder colors while Loretta loved pastels. It showed in how they dressed and in their choice of makeup. But besides that, they had a lot of the same interests, including swimming. They both actively practiced every day as part of a synchronized swim team.

"Anyway," Wanda continued, "the cast will be in the atrium at six tonight for a meet-and-greet and to sign autographs." She pulled at the leather strap of the enormous bag that matched her floral top and began digging. Finally, she pulled out a folder filled with black-and-white headshots. "I made copies of all the cast members that will be on the ship for us to have them sign."

Loretta beamed from ear to ear. "Now you're thinking. Wanda, you're a life saver!"

She handed some to Ruth as well. "I made copies for everyone, including you, Ruth. I have faith you'll watch the show eventually, and you'll be kicking yourself for not getting an autograph. And I wouldn't be a very good friend if I allowed that to happen."

Ruth flipped through the headshots. There were four pictures—two women and two men—and they were all gorgeous. Each the true epitome of a movie star. "I don't know. I just found out I have to make a delivery to Mrs. Wenchester at nine tonight."

Wanda tilted her head. "That old bat still eating Boston Creme Pies every night?"

"Actually, she made the switch to eclairs," Loretta said.

"Eclairs?" Wanda's eyes grew. "What does any of this have to do with the meet-and-greet anyway? Are you worried about time? You'll have plenty of time."

Loretta pointed her thumb at Wanda. "She's right, Ruth."

"And Betty will be there," Wanda offered.

Betty was the librarian aboard the ship who was also part of the gang. Although she didn't drink and party as much as the other women, she often went along with their many adventures. In fact, out of all the women in the gang, Ruth had the most in common with Betty. Betty was a retired English teacher and an avid reader. She read anything she could get her hands on, from books to magazines, newspapers, even the back of shampoo bottles. That's why Ruth found it hard to believe she'd be interested in a soap opera show. "She watches *Darkness into Light?*"

"Huge fan," Wanda said.

Ruth considered it a moment longer. "Okay. I'll be there."

"Good. Then it's a date." Wanda straightened out the papers in the folder, her freshly painted boysenberry fingernails catching the reflection of the yellow lights emanating from the chandeliers above. She slid it back into her over-sized leather duffel bag she called a purse and looked at Loretta. "I have to get back to the salon; it's crazy over there. But I'll see you in the atrium tonight—six o'clock sharp." Then she turned to Ruth. "Don't let me down, Ruth."

Turning on her heels, Wanda waddled away toward the door, but not before grabbing a strawberry shortcake cupcake on her way out.

CHAPTER 3

"Maria, I have to tell you something," said the man on the stage.

Loretta leaned into Ruth's ear and whispered, "That's Rafael Javiera. He plays Romeo." The atrium was packed with starry-eyed women while two of the actors from the hit telenovela, *Darkness into Light,* performed a scene from the show. It had taken no more than thirty minutes for Ruth and Loretta to change out of their work clothes and into something a little more presentable before rushing to meet the gang at the atrium.

From what Ruth had gathered so far, the ravishing, dark-brunette woman, with long legs and a tight, canary-yellow skirt and heels to match, was in love with the handsome man she'd seen pictures of in the Orca Internet Cafe with Loretta. It seemed like the attractive man was about to break up with this beautiful woman named Maria.

"Romeo, what are you trying to say?" Maria asked. The two actors were standing in what looked like a living room with a couch and a house plant, facing each other, their noses just barely touching.

"I can't be with you. My wife, Catalina, is pregnant..." Romeo sighed dramatically. "...with my child."

Maria gasped. "No!" She pulled away from him, tears welling up in her eyes. "That can't be! I need you!"

"Maria," Romeo started, "what about your fiancé, Gustavo?"

"You know I'm only marrying him for the money. So that I can divorce him, and you leave Catalina, and then we can live like royalty together on a private island, like we planned."

"But Gustavo's my brother. I can't do this to him."

Ruth furrowed her eyebrows and glanced over at Loretta and the gang. All the women were leaning forward, completely entranced by the actors. Loretta dabbed her eye with a tissue while Wanda was staring at the stage, her lips moving. Ruth couldn't hear what she was saying, but it looked like she was mouthing, "C'mon, c'mon."

Ruth returned her attention to the actors, unsure if

anyone else was picking up on the fact that this love triangle was a little more than complicated.

On-stage, Maria grabbed Romeo's shoulders. "How can you do this to *him*? What about me? What about our love?"

Romeo bowed his head. "I'm sorry, Maria. I can't."

"You know you love me! Tell me you love me!" she demanded, now clutching his shirt and pulling him in closer to her.

Romeo sighed. "Maria, please."

"Tell me!" Maria yelled, but before Romeo could answer, Maria slapped him across the face. A blonde woman walked in just in time to witness the slap. She gasped.

Maria looked over Romeo's shoulder and saw the woman. "Catalina!"

Catalina's shock quickly turned to rage as she lunged toward Maria. "How dare you touch my husband!"

Then Romeo shouted, "No, Catalina! The baby!" But the two women were already fumbling, clawing at each other.

Ruth couldn't believe what she was watching. She caught movement from the corner of her eye and turned to see Wanda jabbing the air as if she were fighting Catalina. Or was she fighting an imaginary Maria?

Heavy footsteps approaching could be heard on stage.

Romeo turned to the audience and said in a harsh whisper, "Gustavo!" Romeo fled, leaving Catalina and Maria rolling around on the floor.

A man Ruth could only guess was Gustavo walked in, surprised to see two women fighting in the room. "What is going on?" he asked as he pulled Catalina off of his fiancée.

Catalina screamed at Maria as she continued thrashing the air, "Stay away from my husband!"

Gustavo lifted her off her feet from behind as she struggled to break free from his arms. "You stay away from him or I'll kill you," she said. "You hear me, Maria? You'll be dead!"

When Gustavo successfully pulled Catalina off the stage, Maria turned to the audience.

"No, Catalina..." Maria said. She pulled a small vial out from her pocket and held it up between her finger and her thumb. The atrium lights made the contents of the half-filled vial sparkle. "*You're* dead." An evil grin spread across Maria's blood-red lips.

"End scene!" a man with sunglasses and a goatee called from the side. The director, perhaps?

Another middle-aged man approached the atrium's stage. He was pudgy, yet looked sharp in his suit and thick, gold jewelry. "Thank you, everyone, for joining us and watching a live-action performance of *Darkness into Light*. I'm Jay Juan, the producer of the show."

There was a roaring applause and the man paused, waiting for the excitement to die down. Once the clapping ceased, he said, "The next episode will air on television tomorrow at noon. And don't forget to watch the season finale. What will Romeo do? Who will he choose? His wife and baby? Or will he betray his brother, Gustavo, to be with his one true love, Maria?"

"I hope he chooses Maria," Wanda said to Loretta.

"Me too," Loretta said.

Ruth turned to them. "Really? Don't you think he should live up to his vows as a husband and take care of his wife and child?"

Betty shook her head. "This is a telenovela, Ruth. He's supposed to flee to his one true love, even if it means neglecting his responsibilities as a husband. Otherwise, what's the point of watching?"

Wanda nodded. "Yeah! What Betty said."

Loretta agreed.

Feedback from the microphone drew their attention back to the stage. There stood another man, whom Ruth had never seen before. He was thin and seemed to be at least ten years younger than the previous man. She could only assume he was another addition to the *Dark-*

ness into Light crew. "Hi," he started, meekly. "The meet-and-greet will start in a few minutes, so if we can form a line..." Before he could finish his sentence, the crowd began to push forward toward the tables in front of the stage, where four chairs sat empty.

"All right, girls, this is it!" Wanda said, pulling out her folder of headshots from her bag.

"Can you believe it?" Loretta asked, as she got her photos ready. "We're about to meet Rafael Javiera, in person!"

Ruth had her photos in her hand as well, but wasn't quite as excited as the other gals. If anything, she felt more concerned. The crowd around them was getting a little pushy.

Wanda's body suddenly lurched forward a bit. She stumbled slightly and turned her head, shooting a glare at the person behind her. "Hey! Watch it!" She glanced at Loretta, Ruth, and Betty. "People," she muttered, shaking her head.

Just as they were making their way to the front where the tables were, Ruth felt the urge. She and Loretta had been in such a hurry to get to the atrium that she had forgotten to go to the bathroom. Now, suddenly, she had a bit of an emergency on her hands. She decided to try to hold it. How long could a meet-and-greet take? Ruth craned her neck to see over the crowd, but she couldn't see much. Darn her short stature, a curse among the women in the Shores family.

She lifted herself onto her tiptoes, spotting Rafael and the woman who played Maria. They seemed to be the most popular. Every person wanted to take a picture with the two stars. She sighed, knowing the gang would also want pictures. Then, two men arguing to her left caught her attention. She turned to see the producer, Jay, having what seemed like a heated discussion with the director.

Ruth shook her head. It must be very stressful to produce and direct a mega-hit show.

She felt the urge again, only this time, she was pretty sure she was about to have an accident. She regarded Loretta, but her friend was too busy talking to Wanda and Betty.

"...and you'll never guess who came in and made an appointment to get her nails done tonight!" Wanda was saying.

The two women shook their heads.

"Catalina from *Darkness into Light*!"

Both Loretta and Betty were talking over each other, asking Wanda what she was like in person and what she was getting done.

Wanda waved both her hands at them to get them to quiet down. When they calmed down, she continued,

"She is so sweet and kind. And she told us that there is a big surprise ending for the season finale, but she can't tell us what. But..." Wanda paused for dramatic effect, then said, "It's to die for."

The women squealed in delight and Wanda joined them. "Her exact words," she added.

"What's she getting done?" Betty asked.

"Loretta," Ruth said, nudging her friend.

Loretta held up a finger to Ruth, signaling for her to wait.

"Just her nails," Wanda said. "She already has beautiful nails, so she just wants a fresh coat of paint, and she already picked her color."

"What color?" Loretta asked.

"Devilishly Divine Cherry."

Both women swooned. "Isn't that the one with the sparkle in it?" one of them asked.

"It's a subtle sparkle," Wanda replied. "Very subtle. It's got to hit the light just right."

Ruth nudged Loretta again, only harder this time. In her urgency, she didn't care about nail polish.

Loretta turned around. "What is it, Ruth?"

"I have to go to the restroom."

"Now?"

Ruth bounced up and down slightly as if trying to hold it. "Yes."

"But we are so close to Rafael Javiera!"

"Here." Ruth handed her the actors' headshots. "Just hold my stuff. I'll be right back."

Wanda shook her head and said to Loretta and Betty, "She's going to miss it."

Ruth turned and scurried off to the restrooms. She didn't care if she missed it. Nature called, and at her age, she had to answer to it.

She rushed past the crowds and by the stage where the two men were still arguing.

"Seems like you forgot where your place is," she heard the producer say.

The director got up from his chair, and Ruth slowed her pace, watching. "My place?" The man inched closer to the producer's face. "One of these days, Jay," the director started, "someone is going to put you in *your* place, and you better hope it's not me that has to do it, because I'll make sure it's permanent."

As much as Ruth really wanted to see how this played out between the two fellows, she had to go! She felt like she was about to burst.

There were public restrooms in the atrium just past the two men who were arguing. She threw open the doors and scurried to one of the open stalls, her thick two-inch heels clomping against the porcelain floor.

Running into one of the middle stalls, she slammed the door, locking it quickly.

When she was done, she heard the door to the restroom open, and a woman's voice, with a Latina accent, echoed in the small space.

"What!?" the woman asked. "Are you sure?"

There was a moment of silence, and Ruth leaned forward to take a peek out from under the stall. She was surprised to see a pair of canary-yellow stilettos pointing at her. Then the shoes aimed toward the sink area. Ruth pulled herself back up to a sitting position. She'd seen those heels before.

The woman let out a frustrated, guttural sound from the back of her throat. "He's done me wrong for the last time. Wait until I get my hands on him!" The phone clattered and skid across the floor toward Ruth's stall. Ruth could only assume the woman had thrown it in a fit of anger. At first, Ruth was sure it had to be broken, but then she noticed it was encased, so maybe it wasn't. But one thing was sure, the screen was definitely cracked.

The yellow stilettos aimed toward the phone, clicking as they approached. Once they were facing the device, Ruth could see the woman's slender hand pick it up. After the phone disappeared, Ruth heard the sound of the water running at the sink before the clacking of the heels hurried out the door.

Slowly opening the stall door, Ruth made her way to the sink. She looked into the mirror, adjusting herself and combing her thinning hair with her fingers. She wondered what that was about. It was obvious that the woman was very upset.

When Ruth was done at the sink, she walked back out to the line for the meet-and-greet. Her friends were next in line to meet the handsome Rafael Javiera. She quickened her pace, scuttling across the atrium to get back to her friends.

"Hey! No cuts!" a voice called out.

Ruth turned around to see a woman with short silver hair and a lavender hat with flowers. It was Bertie, another crew member, who worked at one of the information desks.

"I was here before," Ruth said. "I just had to run to the bathroom."

"I don't care what you were doing." The woman crossed her arms. "No cuts!"

Loretta stepped up next to Ruth. "She's with me."

"So?"

Wanda, who had just finished up taking a picture with Rafael, trotted over. "Back off, Bertie," Wanda chimed in. Wanda and Bertie hadn't ever gotten along as long as Ruth had known them. Apparently, they had both graduated from the same high school and had a history. Wanda claimed that Bertie tried to steal her boyfriend, several times. Bertie, on the other hand, denied the claims, but always followed up with, "He was my boyfriend first," and "I didn't see a ring on your finger." To which Wanda would snarl like a chihuahua.

"And if I don't?" Bertie challenged.

Wanda stepped up into Bertie's face. They were nose to nose—it was clear neither of them would back down. "Then I'll…"

"Ladies, ladies, please." Rafael Javiera came out from behind the table. "There is plenty of Romeo to go around."

Ruth's brows furrowed. Did this man just refer to himself in the third person? Then she realized he was referring to his character, so she gave him a pass.

The famed actor walked up to Ruth and took her hand. "Well, who is this ravishing young lady?"

Ruth's cheeks flushed.

Rafael smiled at her. "What is your name?"

"Oh…I…I'm…" Ruth suddenly felt warm. She let out a nervous giggle and immediately suppressed the urge to kick herself. What was her problem? Of course, she couldn't remember the last time a young man had called her ravishing—or young, for that matter. "I'm Ruth. Ruth Shores. I'm a baker on the ship and…and so is my friend, Loretta."

Rafael regarded Loretta. "A pleasure to meet you."

Loretta let out a giggle herself. "The pleasure is all mine."

"So, you're both bakers on the ship. That's delightful. I love desserts. What's your specialty?"

Ruth thought for a moment. She didn't know what her specialty was. Baking was her passion, her art, and she couldn't choose. "Cakes?" She suppressed another urge to kick herself.

Rafael let out a chuckle. "Well, I can't wait to try some of your cakes, Ruth. Would you like a picture?"

"I suppose that…"

Rafael, still smiling, put his arm around her shoulder. "Do you have your phone?"

Ruth shook her head.

Loretta stepped up. "I do," she said, pulling out her phone to take a picture.

Ruth smiled, and after Loretta snapped the picture, Ruth hurried over and took her phone. She couldn't help but look at the photo that was just taken. She grimaced when she realized how awkward she looked and said, "Loretta, it's your turn."

Rafael motioned for her to come closer to him so they could take a picture together. "Yes, my dear Loretta. Come. Let's take a picture."

Ruth fumbled with the phone and tried tapping the

screen to take the picture, but she wasn't sure if it took. Loretta must have noticed her confusion and said, "It's the big round button at the bottom of the screen. Tap that."

Ruth did as she was told, and the phone instantly took a snapshot. The picture of Loretta and Rafael came out really nice. Though, Ruth wasn't surprised. Her friend, having been in pageants in her younger days, was still very photogenic.

Rafael regarded both women and said, "Well, it was very nice to meet you both. I'll have to try your cakes sometime soon."

Both of the woman nodded, starry eyed. His smile was bright, and his dark eyes, enchanting.

Once Ruth snapped out of it and broke the spell, she turned to Loretta. "Nice man. Did you want to meet his lover?"

"Maria? No way. I got what I wanted."

Ruth let out a chuckle. They met up with Wanda and Betty as they chattered on about meeting the stars. They went to Cate's Cafe, which was down the hall from the atrium, and paid full price for their gourmet decaf espressos. Many had commented on the idea of Cate's decaf espresso, calling it an oxymoron, but Cate had explained many times that espresso was made with a unique brewing method by forcing water through tightly packed, dark, rich, and freshly ground coffee. A treat none of them minded paying extra for. The Coffee Verdi was their bestseller and it was what they used for the espresso. It was the kind of coffee you inhaled first, it was so divine.

After Ruth finished her espresso, she ordered a decaf coffee. They talked a while longer, except for Wanda, who had already left about a half hour before to get back to work at the salon. But Betty and Loretta were great company, and she enjoyed her hot drink and the conversation. Then Ruth stopped abruptly and looked at her watch. "Oh no!"

"What is it, Ruth?" Loretta asked.

"Mrs. Wenchester! It's almost nine. I have to go. I'm late!"

CHAPTER 4

Making her way back through the atrium, which was now almost completely cleared out from the meet-and-greet, Ruth headed to a side elevator down the hall. Down on the third level, where she was stationed, she hustled down the corridor, passing some of the other staff members on the ship. A few "hey's" and "hi's" echoed as she hurried past them. Once in her cabin, it didn't take her long to get back into her uniform. The saying on the ship among her crewmates was, "We don't get days off, we take hours off," which meant there was more napping than actual sleeping done among the crew, staff, and even the higher-ranked officers. There was no such thing as taking a day off when working for the *Splendor of the Seas*. Not until your contract was up. So,

Ruth had quickly become accustomed to changing her clothes at a moment's notice.

Once she was dressed, out she went, making a beeline for the kitchen. Usually, she worked in the kitchen for the Mermaid's Dinner Room, which she and the staff sometimes referred to as the banquet hall, but she needn't go to deck five to that kitchen. The eclairs were stashed in one of the kitchens down the main corridor, also known as I-95.

Luckily for Ruth, when she made it to the kitchen, Janice was nowhere to be seen. She checked the time and realized she was still several minutes behind. Not too late for most guests, but when it came to Mrs. Wenchester, she might as well have been killing her by starvation.

Ruth quickly set up Mrs. Wenchester's dessert on a tray with paper doilies and covered it with a stainless-steel dome cover. She carted the tray down the hall and into the elevator. Once inside, she hit the button for deck sixteen and adjusted her name tag, trying to calm her nerves.

There were only a handful of people from the staff that could deliver Mrs. Wenchester's food. She'd either offended, threatened, or refused to open the door to just about everyone. Loretta was one of those people, after an incident where Mrs. Wenchester called Loretta a derogatory name that would make a sailor blush. It had set Loretta on edge, and she'd fired back, calling the woman an old, miserable hag. Surely, it was unlike Loretta to say such a horrible thing, especially to a guest—but luckily for her, after many complaints among staff, including Janice herself, Loretta was let off with a warning. But, unfortunately for Ruth, the old woman could tolerate her, barely.

Ruth reached Mrs. Wenchester's door and took a deep breath before knocking. It always took Ruth a few moments to mentally prepare for the woman who caused more grief than trying to assemble a croquembouche.

The door opened and Mrs. Wenchester stood there. She wasn't at all intimidating with her Estelle Getty haircut and stature, but her icy, blue eyes were cold, and she bore a scowl that seemed to be permanently printed on her face. She held her yappy little Yorkie named Isabella, who was dressed in a pink fur coat. The dog tensed, sneering and letting out a low grumble aimed directly at Ruth.

The only two modes that dog had were warning or attack. All it did was grumble, growl, and strike. One time, a woman named Carla had tried to deliver Mrs. Wenchester's dinner, and the dog pounced on her ankle and wouldn't let go. Rumor had it, Beno, another crew member who'd been walking past, happened to hear Carla's shrieks and came in. He tried to pull the dog off of Carla's leg while Mrs. Wenchester beat him over the head with her cane, screaming for him to take his grimy little hands off her Isabella. He had finally pulled Isabella off Carla, but not without Isabella successfully tearing a good chunk of her pant-leg off. Ruth couldn't help but imagine Isabella stashing the piece of torn fabric somewhere for keepsake, like a souvenir.

Usually, the ship didn't allow pets onboard, but apparently, someone up the ranks had given this horrid woman a pass.

"You're late," the old woman said. Isabella echoed her owner's temper, letting out a yip.

"Sorry, Mrs. Wenchester. I—"

"Save it."

Ruth jerked her head back slightly at Mrs. Wenchester's short, verbal blow.

Mrs. Wenchester stepped aside, allowing Ruth to wheel in her dessert. "You trying to starve a poor old lady?"

"No, Mrs. Wenchester." Ruth stopped. "Of course not. I'm only four minutes late."

"Late is late." Mrs. Wenchester stroked Isabella's head. "Otherwise, what's the point of a clock if people are just going to do whatever, whenever, all willy nilly?"

"I understand, Mrs. Wenchester." Ruth looked around. "Where would you like me to place your dessert tonight?"

"Over there." Mrs. Wenchester pointed to the balcony window.

Ruth pushed the cart toward the window and lifted the plate, placing it on the table. "There you are. Now you can watch the ocean while you eat."

"Bah!" Mrs. Wenchester bent over, putting Isabella on the floor. Ruth eyed the dog, making sure it didn't charge after her ankle. Instead, it cocked its head at Ruth and then scuttled across the floor to its big, pink bed with ruffles. The words "Queen Isabella" were stitched in pink across the front of the bed.

"I don't need to see the ocean," Mrs. Wenchester continued. "I see enough of that."

Ruth didn't know what to say. So, she offered her default response to guests: "Very well, ma'am." She grabbed the cart and turned it to face the door. "If you need anything—"

"Yeah, yeah," Mrs. Wenchester waved her off.

Ruth gave the woman a curt nod and started for the door, wheeling the cart in front of her. As she passed Isabella's bed, the small Yorkie glared at her. Her tiny head slowly swiveled, following Ruth's trek to the exit. Ruth reciprocated with a side stare. There was no telling what the little mongrel would do, but Ruth sensed she was plotting her attack.

When Ruth reached the door, Mrs. Wenchester let out a blood-curdling scream. Isabella bolted up on all fours, and Ruth whipped around. In that split second, she saw what looked like a body hurtle down past Mrs. Wenchester's balcony window. It ended with a splash below. Isabella began to bark incessantly, and Ruth noticed Mrs. Wenchester begin to sway. She left the cart and ran up behind the old woman, catching her before she hit the floor.

CHAPTER 5

Ruth lay Mrs. Wenchester down gently on the floor. Isabella was next to her, now whining in apprehension.

Ruth hurried to the balcony window and opened it, peering down just in time to see a body floating on the water. A person overboard usually didn't end well.

Running over to Mrs. Wenchester's phone, Ruth hit the emergency button and dialed a four-digit number. When she heard a "click," she said, "Code Oscar…uh…at the stern. I repeat, Code Oscar!" She hung up the phone to attend to Mrs. Wenchester. The old woman began to stir and her eyes fluttered open. When she came to her senses, she shot Ruth a glare that could bore a hole through a hatched door.

"Get your hands off of me!"

KILLER CAST & DEADLY SPLASH

"Mrs. Wenchester, you fainted. Let me help you."

"I don't need your help." Mrs. Wenchester began to pull herself to her feet.

"You shouldn't get up. You should stay lying down."

"Now you're telling me what to do? You half-witted fool!"

Ruth gave up. She half expected Mrs. Wenchester to faint again getting up too soon, but decided if she had enough blood flowing to her head to insult her that she would be fine. Besides, it seemed like she had forgotten what she'd seen, which was probably best. Ruth decided to play along.

"You're right, Mrs. Wenchester." Ruth got to her feet.

"Where's my cane? Did you steal it?"

"No," Ruth said. "It's right here." Ruth picked up the cane but was slightly hesitant to give it to her. What if she tried cracking her over the head with it? The woman didn't seem to be altogether in the head. Before she could come to a decision, Mrs. Wenchester snatched the cane from Ruth's hands.

"What are you doing? I'd like to have my eclair before it gets stale." Isabella let out another bark toward Ruth, as if echoing Mrs. Wenchester's sentiments. "You can see yourself out now." She pointed to the door with her cane.

"Yes, ma'am," Ruth said, grabbing the cart and

strolling to the door. "Enjoy your late-night snack, Mrs. Wenchester."

Mrs. Wenchester grunted in response as Ruth made her way back to the cart and out the suite. When she closed the door behind her, she exhaled sharply. What had she just seen? Was it real? Had she really seen a body fall from one of the upper decks? Ruth's mind spun. She parked the cart parallel to the wall next to Mrs. Wenchester's cabin and took off down the hall to the elevator.

The humming of the engines had ceased while Ruth was on the elevator. That's when it had dawned on her that the emergency was real and not some figment of her imagination. She wasn't sure which level to get off at and opted for deck fifteen. When she got off the elevator, she hurried across the lounge area to the door that led outside.

There was a crowd of people standing on the first open deck. People were murmuring, and others were staring and pointing over the railing off to the left toward the back of the ship. Ruth made her way through the crowd to the railing and peered over. There were lights and men with life vests and boats. Ruth squinted, trying to get a better look. A dark, man-sized heap covered with a blanket lay on one of the yellow, inflatable boats. A man sitting upright on the boat gave the signal to bring him in. Unlike security, the rescue workers were quick and seemed to be very organized.

Still, Ruth couldn't believe her eyes. Then she overheard a man talking to a group of people behind her, off to her right.

"A man fell overboard from one of the balconies on deck seventeen."

Ruth walked over to the man, who was pointing upward. "Where did you hear that?"

The man turned toward Ruth. "I didn't hear it," the man said. "I just came from there. My wife and I have one of the suites on that deck and there's a slew of security and men in uniforms there. I just came down here to get a better look."

Before the man could say anything more, Ruth was heading back to the elevator. When she made it to the seventeenth level, the doors opened. There were men and women everywhere, wearing uniforms with numerous stripes on their shoulders. She sifted through the people to get to the cabin that was open, where people were filing in and out. As she approached the threshold, a familiar officer was coming out of the room, his potbelly guiding him. He had a white Styrofoam cup in his left hand, and he held out his free hand, shielding her from coming in. "Oh, no, Ruth. This cabin is off limits." She could smell the stale coffee on his breath. A small brown coffee stain lingered just below his gold name tag that read, "Chief Security Officer, Harry J. Humphrey."

"What happened?"

"A man went overboard." Officer Humphrey took a deep breath. "Unfortunately, we just got word—he didn't survive."

Ruth gasped. "Oh no! That's horrible!"

Humphrey gave her a confused look. "Weren't you one of the crew members that called in the Code Oscar?"

"I did. I just happened to see a body falling outside Mrs. Wenchester's balcony window while delivering her evening eclair."

"I thought she gets a slice of Boston Cream Pie every night."

Ruth furrowed her eyebrows. "How do you know that?"

"I know more than you think." He tapped his forehead with his index finger. Then he shrugged. "Besides, everyone knows that."

"Well, now she wants an eclair."

Humphrey nodded. "Can't say the woman doesn't

have good taste," he said, rubbing his protruding belly. "Either way, whether you saw the body or not, you can't come in here."

"May I at least know which of the guests has fallen victim? I want to be able to regard their family or friends with the utmost sympathy."

"Hm." Humphrey scratched his chin. Then he twisted his entire body, regarding a tall, red-haired man talking to another fellow stripe behind him in the room. "Officer Malloy, do you have the victim's name?"

It took everything within Ruth to not roll her eyes. Leave it to Humphrey to remember what Mrs. Wenchester ordered for dessert but not the victim whom he was currently investigating.

Malloy turned toward Humphrey. "It's Jay Juan."

The name sounded familiar. Then Ruth's eyes grew wide when she realized where she'd heard it. She regarded the man from the hallway. "You mean the producer of *Darkness into Light*?"

The man nodded. "Yup. That's the one."

CHAPTER 6

Humphrey conducted a brief interview of what exactly Ruth saw, while officers hurried about. There wasn't much to the story. Ruth explained that she had only caught a glimpse of a man falling past the window.

"It happened in a flash," Ruth said.

"What about Mrs. Wenchester?"

"Mrs. Wenchester fainted. But when she came to, she didn't seem to remember anything. She was back to her old self again, if you know what I mean."

"I'll have to check on her." Humphrey didn't seem to catch her drift about Mrs. Wenchester's crab-apple personality.

Ruth arched an eyebrow. "It's her bedtime. She doesn't like being disturbed at odd hours of the night."

"I have to make sure she's all right and see if she remembers anything."

Ruth shook her head, knowing that his good intentions were a bad idea. "Good luck to you, sir," Ruth said loosely.

Just then, Officer Malloy walked over to them. "Excuse me, sir."

Humphrey regarded him. "What is it, Marvin?"

Malloy was holding a folder as he walked over to Humphrey. He looked at Ruth and whispered in Humphrey's ear, handing him the folder. Humphrey opened it and stared at whatever was inside for a few seconds before nodding and closing it. "Thank you, Officer Malloy."

Giving a curt nod with his hands clasped behind his back, Malloy made his way out, acknowledging Ruth once more before he left.

When he was out of sight, Ruth motioned to the folder. "What's going on?"

"Nothing, really. Apparently, there was a nasty bump on the victim's forehead, by his temple."

Ruth drew in a sharp breath. "You think foul play?"

Humphrey shook his head. "He could have received the wound during his fall or during impact." Then he eyed Ruth. "Don't get any ideas."

Ruth was taken back by his comment. She put her hand to her chest. "Me? What ideas?"

"I don't need another repeat of what happened before." Ruth knew he was referring to the last time there was foul play on the ship. Humphrey began to pace. "Last thing we need is another murder on the ship. So, there is no need to jump to conclusions. Accidents happen."

Ruth nodded. "I understand." But Ruth didn't. She knew it was a straight fall from that particular balcony to the water. And the ocean was so deep, it wasn't like he would hit his head on the ocean floor. No, there was no way this was an accident. But what if she was wrong?

Humphrey stopped pacing and turned to face Ruth. "For now, he will be resting in the ship's morgue until we can transport his body. I'll need to contact his family." He rubbed his forehead, obviously stressed. "That's never an easy phone call."

Ruth felt sorry for Humphrey. His job couldn't be easy.

After the interview, Humphrey escorted Ruth back to her cabin. She wasn't sure if he was just trying to be a gentleman or if he was doing it to make sure she didn't get herself into trouble, digging for answers and investigating like she had the last time there was a death on the ship.

When she got to her room, she noticed Loretta wasn't there. She'd either be at the casino with Wanda, Betty, and the gang, drinking and gambling, or she'd found out that the producer of her beloved show had gone overboard.

But how could that have happened? Last time a man went overboard, he'd been completely drunk and was pretending to be Rose from *Titanic*, standing on the second rung of the railing with his arms stretched out as if he were flying. The man had survived, thankfully, but at the time, it was terrifying. It was well known on the ship that people who fell overboard usually didn't live to tell the tale of their unfortunate mishap.

What about Jay Juan? The last time she'd seen the man, he didn't seem to be drunk. Not even tipsy. Of course, he'd been in a heated argument with the director. What had the man said to Jay? Something about putting him in his place permanently? Hardly a death threat, but the director definitely didn't seem to like Jay.

Ruth let out a big yawn and looked at the time. It was way past her bedtime, and she was more than exhausted after a long and eventful, yet tragic, day. Of course, it was unlikely tomorrow was going to be any easier. Deciding to get ready for bed, she changed into her nightwear, washed up, and brushed her teeth. She slipped in between the covers of her bed, allowing her muscles to relax and for the tension in her body to melt away as she drifted off to sleep.

Ruth felt like she had just closed her eyes when someone jostled her. Then, she heard a voice off in the distance, as if she were standing at one end of a long corridor and the voice was coming from the other. At first, the voice was muffled, but within seconds, it got louder and clearer.

"Come on, Ruth. Wake up!"

It was Loretta. Once Ruth came to her senses, she opened her eyes.

Loretta stepped back and put her hands on her hips. "Finally," she said, then walked over to the mirror at the tiny desk between their beds. "Did you hear?"

Ruth sat up, rubbed her eyes, and let out a long, much-needed yawn. "What?"

Loretta swiveled herself toward Ruth. "Jay Juan is dead!"

"Did you know him?"

"No. Not personally, but you know, he's the producer of *Darkness into Light*." Loretta faced the mirror. "Oh, this is just so awful. I can't believe someone would murder him."

Ruth shot up into a sitting position on her bed. "Murdered?" She pulled the covers from her legs and got up. "He was murdered? How do you know?"

"Are you serious? Of course, it was murder. It had to be. Think about it, Ruth. The man was producing one of the biggest shows in the world."

Ruth dropped her shoulders and gave her friend a skeptical look. "The world?" she asked, highlighting her friend's exaggeration.

Loretta looked at Ruth through the mirror. "Yes, Ruth. The world. He would never commit suicide."

"What if it was an accident?"

Loretta spun around in her chair. "An accident? No way. It had to be murder. So many people could have wanted him dead. They probably thought they could just toss him overboard, and he'd be long gone. No body, no evidence."

"I spoke to Officer Humphrey last night about it."

Loretta looked at Ruth. "What did he say?"

"He said it was an accident."

"I find that hard to believe." Loretta faced the desk, opening the drawer and pulling out her moisturizer. "You know Humphrey is going to do everything in his power to downplay this. Especially after the first two murders." She rubbed a thin layer of the cream into her face, focusing on the T-zone area. "Did he say anything else?"

"Yes," Ruth said, almost immediately regretting it as soon as the word escaped her lips. There was no turning back now. "There was a bump on his head. But that doesn't mean it was a murder."

"But it's possible," Loretta said. "Hey, you solved the last murder. Maybe you can solve this one."

"No one said this was a murder."

"I am."

Ruth shook her head. "Loretta, if someone claims or if there's evidence it was murder, we'll look into it. But if we don't hurry and get to work, Janice will have us in body bags, and that will be one very quick murder to solve."

Loretta nodded, getting up from the desk, and they both scurried to get ready for work. As they walked down the hallway toward the kitchen, Loretta came up with several different scenarios of how Jay might have been murdered that were completely outrageous. Ruth didn't entertain any of Loretta's crazy theories with a response.

They walked in through the doors to find all of the cooking and baking staff huddled in a large group, chattering. No one seemed to notice Ruth and Loretta's presence. Then the baker in charge of the early morning buffet desserts said, "What if someone didn't like the way the script was written and, you know…" The woman dragged her finger across her throat.

"I think someone offed him because of money," one of the cooks said. "Those producers make a lot of money, especially if they are working on a hit TV show."

"I heard it was the co-executive producer. Think about it. He'd be next in line to take his job."

Loretta nudged Ruth in an effort to prove that a group of people talking about the incident as if it were already proclaimed a murder validated her claims. Ruth had to admit, it did conjure up suspicion within herself. Though, she had to stop it before—

Janice burst through the door, clipboard in hand. "What is going on in here?"

Everyone stopped and looked at Janice. The room was instantly quiet; they could've heard a mouse sneeze.

"We have work to do," Janice continued.

The woman in charge of the early morning dessert buffet spoke up. "There was an M.O.B. last night."

"Man overboard?" Janice shook her head. "That is not for us to busy ourselves with. Our job is to give the guests who are still on this ship the best experience and bake delicious treats. Now, fire up those ovens!"

The crowd dispersed, hustling to get their list of

pastries and cakes started. And with that, Janice was stomping out the door.

Why hadn't Janice confronted her about allowing all the chatter? Ruth was the head pastry chef, after all. Casting that thought aside, Ruth and Loretta hurried to their own station, gathering the utensils they needed to start the Piña Colada cupcakes and the Sangria cakes for those who didn't like coconut but still want to party. John wouldn't be in for a few more hours. He took the later shift, while Ruth and Loretta were natural early birds.

Ruth couldn't keep her mind from wandering, quickly grasping onto what one of the baking staff had just said. What if someone didn't like how the script was written? Her thoughts went to the movie *Misery*, and she shuddered. Crazed fans did exist. Or what if the co-executive producer did want to off the producer to take over the mega-hit show?

Loretta was snapping her fingers. "Earth to Ruth."

Ruth shook the thoughts away. "What?"

Loretta jutted out her hip and placed her fist upon it. "Are you thinking about the M.O.B.? I told you something's fishy about it."

"I don't know. Maybe you're right, Loretta. Perhaps there was someone behind the producer's death. Maybe it was murder."

"What do you propose we do?"

"Speak with those closest to him. If there was foul play, someone in his circle has to know something about it, and people are usually bad at keeping secrets, especially when pushed."

"So, you're saying…"

"We'll have to keep our eyes and ears open."

CHAPTER 7

Later that day, Ruth was roaming around the ship, trying to find Loretta, whom she had lost sometime between working on the presentation of the desserts and helping the waitstaff. Though, she was also keeping an eye out for any of the stars from the telenovela show. She didn't know anything about them, and they hadn't shown up at the banquet hall. Perhaps they were still mourning the producer who had just passed.

She'd checked the kitchen and the bathrooms, then she went to their cabin, but it was empty and quiet. Maybe Loretta had gone to the pool to do some laps since she hadn't gone that morning, probably due to the shock of the producer that had gone overboard the night before. But Loretta wasn't at the pool either.

Ruth went up to one of the outside decks to see if Loretta was with their favorite bartender, Geoff. He wore a colorful tee under his mandatory work vest, which made him look not only approachable but fun. A tall man with sandy-blond hair and big but perfectly aligned teeth, he had a bright smile that could be seen miles away. Ruth was always happy to see him and figured everyone felt that way about Geoff. He had a personality that attracted most people and a vibe that not only made one feel easy but had a certain warmth and familiarity to it.

She approached him. "Hey, Geoff. Have you seen Loretta?"

He wiped a glass with a white towel, then hung the glass above his head. "Sorry, Ruth. I haven't seen her at all today."

Ruth hopped up on one of the stools. She was so short, her feet didn't touch the ground. Though, it was all right with her. Her feet were aching after a long day. "Do you know the telenovela show, *Darkness into Light*?"

"Sure do. The stars are on the ship to shoot the season finale on Mermaid's Cay." He grabbed another wet glass from the counter. "I do hope that Romeo and Maria run away together."

Ruth raised an eyebrow. Was she living in an alternate universe? What was it about this show that had everyone hooked? "That seems to be everyone's sentiments toward that love triangle."

Geoff was rotating the towel around the inside of the glass. "Well, they do have quite a history."

"Have you seen anyone from the show roaming around?"

Geoff shook his head. "Though, Maria stopped by last night for a few drinks. Got herself a little tipsy." He let out a chuckle.

"When?"

Geoff shifted his gaze upward, thinking. "Oh, I'd say around nine thirty. She stuck around for a couple hours."

Ruth thought about the night before. The M.O.B. was sometime after 9 p.m.—quarter after nine, Ruth remembered.

"Did she say anything?"

"Uh," Geoff started. "Not much. After a few drinks, she said something about a man getting what he deserved."

Ruth perked up. "Anything else?"

"Yeah, there was more, but it was mostly incoherent. I mean, she was drunk."

Ruth hopped off the stool. "Thanks, Geoff."

"Don't you want a drink?"

"Not now. I'll be back for one, though."

Geoff nodded. "See you later, then, Ruth!" he shouted to her as she hurried away.

Now she was more determined to find Loretta. She went back inside, passing the Sunset Bar and Grille. As she walked, the smell of a sizzling burger lingered just outside the doorway and it made her stomach growl. She would have gone inside, but she decided to head to the crew's mess hall. Though the burgers at the Sunset Bar and Grille were definitely fresher and better, the mess hall would be significantly cheaper. Maybe Loretta was there. If she had gone swimming after work, she would have built up quite an appetite.

Ruth took the elevator, making her way down to the lower deck where the crew basically lived on the ship, and she navigated through the maze of corridors toward the mess hall. As she passed the staff lounge, she heard people speaking Spanish. She opened the door and spotted not only Loretta but the gang, which included Wanda, Betty, and Flossie, who was a cashier at the gift shop. She was a very quiet lady who usually just went with the flow, hardly ever opposing the other ladies in the gang.

They were all sitting next to one another watching *Darkness into Light*. None of them even acknowledged her. Their eyes were glued to the TV set.

Rafael—aka Romeo—was on the screen, caressing

Maria's cheek. "I can't be apart from you," he said to her. "You are my one true love, Maria." Maria was more stunning in person, but even on TV, she had the most gorgeous long hair that hung in loose waves. She looked like she could've been a model for Finesse hair shampoo.

Maria gently stroked his wrist and then she grasped his hand, holding it to her face. Her eyes closed, and she said, "But, Romeo, what if he finds out?"

"Don't worry. Nothing can stand in the way of true love."

The couple moved in slowly toward each other, and they went into a dramatic kiss.

Ruth could hear a couple of the women swoon and sigh. She returned her attention to the television screen.

As Romeo and Maria's passionate kiss continued, there was a knock on the door. Maria pulled away from Romeo. "Oh no. It's my husband! Romeo, you must hide!"

Romeo whipped his head from side to side, looking for a good place to hide. He spotted a plant and hid behind it. Maria shook her head. "No, Romeo. The coat closet!"

Romeo dashed to the closet, closing the door behind him.

"How can you all watch this?" Ruth asked.

"Hey, you read romance novels," Loretta said, crossing her arms. "I'm sure this isn't much different."

"They're more realistic and less dramatic."

"I love drama," Betty said, pushing her over-sized glasses up the bridge of her nose.

Flossie said, "I know, I can't get enough!"

"And Romeo!" Loretta added.

"He's so dreamy," Wanda said. "I could stare into those dark, walnut eyes all day!"

"And his hair," Betty chimed in.

The women agreed in unison.

Ruth furrowed her eyebrows. "Why is it called *Darkness into Light* anyway?"

"Darkness, like dark secrets," Loretta started.

"Or affairs," Wanda said.

Loretta nodded in agreement. "Yeah, like dark secrets or affairs that are brought to light and cause all the drama."

Ruth shook her head. "I think I'll just stick to my romance novels."

John moseyed in, a bagel sandwich in one hand, chomping away. He turned his head to the TV set. "Oh, *Darkness into Light*. Love this show."

Ruth's mouth dropped. "What? Not you, too?"

John swallowed another bite of his sandwich, taking a seat next to Wanda. He pointed to the screen. "You know, it's funny, I just heard that the co-executive producer, Hector, writes all the episodes, but Jay got all the credit."

Ruth and Loretta exchanged glances. Ruth stepped over to John. "What?"

John stopped chewing and looked back and forth between Ruth and Loretta, who were both staring at him. He looked around, seeming to realize that all the women from the gang were staring at him as well. "Um, what?"

"Come on, out with it, John," Ruth coaxed.

John gave a confused look. "Out with what?"

"Who told you about Hector writing the show and Jay getting the credit?"

"And where?" Loretta added.

"I don't know. I don't remember," John said. "There are a lot of rumors going around, and it's hard to keep them straight."

"Well now, think!" Ruth urged.

John looked up to the ceiling, thinking. "I don't remember. I was just chilling, having a few drinks on one of the upper decks, and this guy next to me told me."

"Did you get a name?" Loretta asked.

John snapped his fingers several times, as if that

would increase his ability to think. "Ted. No, uh, Fred something..."

Ruth and Loretta looked at each other, confused. Then Betty said, "Oh, you mean Frederick Scott?"

"That's it!" John said.

"Frederick Scott?" Ruth asked, then she and Loretta looked at each other again before directing their curious gazes toward Betty. "Who's that?" Ruth asked.

"The director," Betty answered. "He was at the meet-and-greet."

Ruth nodded and returned her gaze to John, who was watching the television screen. "So, what all did this Frederick Scott say?"

John shrugged. "Just what I told you." John craned his neck to see the TV over Ruth's and Loretta's heads. Then he waved his hand, motioning for them to move to the side. "You're blocking my view."

Ruth glanced at Loretta. "I guess we have to pay this Frederick Scott a visit."

CHAPTER 8

"So, how are we going to find this director, Frederick Scott?" Loretta asked. She was dipping the small brush from her nail polish into the little pansy-pink bottle. When it was soaked in paint, she wiped the brush on the side to remove the excess.

Ruth cocked her head. "Do you have to do that in the cabin? It's not like I can open a window, you know." The lower deck where the crew members resided was below sea level, which meant no port holes.

Loretta carefully applied a thin layer of paint to her pinky finger. "Yes. My nails are chipped."

"I thought Wanda does your nails in the salon."

"She started charging more." Loretta put the brush back into the bottle, then lifted her hand, blowing on her wet nails. Turning to Ruth, she wrinkled her forehead. "And now she's demanding tips."

Ruth wasn't surprised. Wanda did passengers', as well as crew members', hair and nails. She usually gave discounts to her friends and some of the crew members, and though she always did a great job and was passionate about her work, it seemed like that passion was now coming with a price.

Loretta twisted the brush's handle, tightening the bottle closed. Then she analyzed her work. "I don't need her. I can do my own nails."

Ruth shook her head. "So, I spoke to Geoff. He said Maria was at his bar last night around 9:30 p.m."

Loretta stopped and looked up at Ruth. "No way! That's right after Jay went…you know…kerplunk."

"I know. That's what I was thinking." Ruth looked at her watch. "It's almost nine now. I could go back to Geoff's bar and see if she returns. In the meantime, maybe you could see if you can find the director guy."

"Frederick Scott." Loretta nodded. She reached into the drawer, pulled out a pouch, and opened it.

"Those are my pearl earrings, Loretta."

Loretta fished out the earrings. "They match my new nail polish."

Ruth couldn't argue. They were an exact match.

"Besides," Loretta continued, "they're not real pearls and they're clip-ons."

Ruth sighed. "Fine, but if you lose them, I'll make sure *you* go 'kerplunk.' My granddaughter, Emma, gave me those."

Loretta was already clipping them onto her earlobes in the mirror. "Seems like a sweet girl. And don't worry, I won't lose them. If I do, I'll throw myself overboard."

Ruth grimaced at her last statement. Too soon, she thought, but then again, Ruth had started it. "All right, and then we'll meet here by midnight."

Loretta groaned. "Can't we make it 11 p.m.? I need my beauty rest."

"Fine. Eleven it is."

"Great!" Loretta got up and strode toward the door. "I guess I'll be off, then." She flipped her pastel pink scarf over her shoulder and strode out the door, Ruth behind her, shaking her head. They shared an elevator to deck fifteen where all the outside amenities were, including Geoff's bar. When the doors slid open, they got off, going their separate ways.

Ruth took the door leading to the outside deck where Geoff's bar was.

As she approached, Geoff waved gleefully. "Would you like a Perfect Cosmopolitan?" he asked as she boosted herself up onto one of the stools.

"You read my mind, Geoff."

He smiled at her as he grabbed a glass, twirling it in the air. He was a regular showman when it came to preparing drinks. It was another reason his bar was never without a crowd of patrons. Many times, all the seats were taken, and Ruth would have to wait to get a drink. But, in her opinion, he was the best bartender on the ship. Not only did many of the passengers agree with her, but so did the crew and staff.

When he was done making her drink, he grabbed a napkin, placing it down before setting her drink on top of it. He waited as she took a sip, something he did with many of his customers. He took great pride in his work, or as he would call it, his creations.

She tasted the Cosmo and rolled her eyes, letting out a sigh of approval. "Geoff, I swear, when I don't think it's even possible, you somehow always outdo yourself. This is incredible." She wasn't exaggerating. The drink swept her into a state of oblivion.

Geoff grinned. "I'm glad you like it, Ruth."

"'Like' is an understatement."

Just then, Ruth could hear the rhythmic clicking of high heels approaching.

Geoff looked past Ruth. "I think you're in luck. The guest of honor is on her way."

Ruth turned around to see Maria and, without much

thought, involuntarily looked at her shoes, noticing that they were canary yellow. The same canary-yellow heels she'd been wearing on stage during the meet-and-greet. Then it hit Ruth. They were also the same canary-yellow shoes she had seen in the bathroom. She was the woman who had been talking on the phone.

Ruth turned back around on her stool to face the bar. Geoff was leaning on the bar with both hands on either side, holding himself up. He pulled himself upright and said, "I think I'll leave you to it."

Ruth gave him a nod as he walked to the other side of the bar to help another customer. Then the clacking of the heels stopped, and Ruth could hear someone ask Maria for her autograph.

"Name?" she heard Maria ask. She didn't seem as enthusiastic as her partner Rafael. He didn't even break out of his role as Romeo.

"Amy."

"There," Maria said coldly.

"Thank you, thank you," the fan said.

There were three more heavy clicks of her heels before Maria slapped her hand onto the bar right next to Ruth. Immediately, Ruth noticed her diamond ring glimmering from the bright lights that surrounded them on the deck. Though, it was very hard to miss a huge rock like that.

Maria leaned over the bar, turning her head to the right toward the bartender, who was just finishing a drink for someone at the other end of the bar. "Geoff," she shouted down to him. He turned to her. "Give me your strongest."

Geoff gave her a curt nod and began to work on a drink, scooping ice into a shaker.

Maria slipped onto the stool next to Ruth, tugging at the bottom of the skirt that hugged her thighs.

"Long day?" Ruth asked.

Maria rolled her eyes and turned to Ruth. "Don't tell me you want an autograph, too."

Ruth shook her head. "I don't watch the show."

Maria chuckled. "Right," she said, in genuine disbelief.

"You don't believe me?" Ruth asked.

"Not really. I mean, it's only the best show on TV. Everyone has seen at least an episode. It's like that reality show, *The Rich and Famous Life*."

"Never saw that either. I don't watch much TV. I'd rather read."

Maria's forehead wrinkled. Then she laughed.

Geoff plopped down a glass on the counter in front of her. She picked it up and grasped the stirring straw with her finger and thumb, then took a sip. "You're funny."

"I don't try to be," Ruth said. There was a moment of awkward silence. Then Ruth continued, "I heard what happened to the producer of the show. What a tragedy."

"I wouldn't call it that," Maria said, setting her drink back down on the bar.

Ruth cocked her head. "No? What would you call it, then?"

Maria shrugged. "You ever hear the saying, 'you reap what you sow'?"

"Of course."

"The man was a shyster. Nobody liked him."

Ruth arched an eyebrow. "Oh? Like who?"

"Like everyone. I think he had wronged everyone in one way or another."

"How did he wrong you?"

Maria turned to Ruth. "Me?" She pointed to herself and let out a chuckle. "He couldn't wrong me. I knew who he was beforehand. Before I took the job and became *Maria Melendez*." Maria's accent became thicker as she said her stage name. She picked up her drink and took another sip. "I made sure he didn't wrong me."

"So, what's going to happen to the show?"

"Nothing. Everything is as planned to move forward. The network already put too much money into this trip and to reserve the island for the shoot. And besides, it's the season finale. They have a contract to honor, and the viewers would probably riot if it wasn't shot and aired. They need a conclusion. It's what they've been waiting for."

"Then who is going to take over for Jay?"

"The co-executive producer, Hector, of course. The man was writing most of the scenes anyway." A mischievous smile spread across Maria's red lips. "Though Jay was getting all the credit."

So, the rumor was true. First the director, Frederick Scott, said it, and now Maria. This gave Hector motive—good motive to get rid of Jay. The only question was, did he have opportunity?

"Let's just say that I'm not that heartbroken that Hector will be taking over as producer." Maria took another sip of her drink.

Ruth mirrored her, downing a few large gulps of her own drink. There was another question pressing on Ruth's mind, and she would need the extra alcohol to ask it. "I heard you in the bathroom yesterday, several hours before Jay's death. You said someone had 'done you wrong.' Those exact words. And you said it was time to finish him."

Maria put down her glass and stared intensely at Ruth.

Ruth continued, "Were you talking about Jay Juan?"

Maria finally broke her stare and hopped off the stool. "I don't know what you are talking about." She picked up her drink and downed the rest of it. "I think it's time for me to find another bar," she said, and walked away.

CHAPTER 9

Ruth couldn't believe the response she'd gotten from Maria. The woman had only made herself look more suspicious. What if she was throwing Hector under the bus to steer the attention away from herself? Ruth looked at her watch. It was almost 10:30 p.m. Geoff was busy at the other end of the bar, chatting and laughing. He was showing off his juggling skills while mixing a couple's drink. They were having a great time, and she didn't want to interrupt. Besides, she needed time to herself to work through the conversation she'd just had with the star, and by the time she'd get back to the cabin, it would be close to eleven anyway, the time Ruth and Loretta agreed to meet.

Ruth got up from the bar and began making her way to the elevator. Had Maria been referring to Jay when she threatened him? She had used the same phrasing when describing Jay as she did about the man she was talking about on the phone. And who was she talking to when she was in the bathroom? These were all questions she couldn't figure out without more information. And Maria was definitely hiding something. If it wasn't Jay who she'd been talking about on the phone, wouldn't she have just been honest and said so?

The doors to the elevator slid open, revealing a bare corridor and the distant hum of the engines. She walked down the empty hall, only passing one other staff member who gave her an exhausted hello. He was definitely a newbie, and she smiled as she said hello back, hoping to brighten his night. Though, being a newbie once herself, she knew how hard the first few weeks of working on the cruise line could be with training and orientations. Not to mention, altering your sleep cycle to fit your new schedule. The break in the circadian rhythm could be brutal to the mind and body. Though, it would only take a good night's rest for the poor chap to liven up again, and after those first couple of weeks, he'd be used to it and would have more time for naps.

Ruth opened the door to her cabin. When she closed

it behind her, she took a deep breath and kicked off her shoes. It would be a little while before Loretta came back, and Ruth couldn't wait to take a hot shower.

She went into the bathroom and began to clean her face, stripping away her makeup so she wouldn't look like a sad raccoon when she stepped out of the shower. The bathroom was small, and she always had a hard time balancing all of her beauty products on the tiny sink, often finding herself knocking things over. Then she would have to watch so she didn't whack her head on something as she retrieved the fallen item. It was hard to breathe in there, and it felt like the walls were closing in at times. It was the first time in her life she could say that she might have a better understanding of how it must feel to be claustrophobic.

But her cabinmate didn't seem to have all those problems. Loretta used just as many products as Ruth, maybe more, and she'd never seemed to be bothered by the lack of space. Ruth never heard a clatter or a thud. Instead, the only thing Ruth ever heard was Loretta's off-key singing as she got ready.

Ruth started the shower, and once the water temperature was to her liking, hot and steamy, she slowly stepped in, allowing the hot water to gradually take over and ease her muscles. After a few minutes of just standing there, internally groaning, she began to vigorously wash her hair with her favorite almond, coconut, & papaya-scented shampoo. When she was done in the shower, she dressed into her pajamas and grabbed a robe. Loretta would be back any moment.

Ruth grabbed her lavender lotion and took a seat on the bed. Once she was comfortable, she began applying the lotion to her arms. Since she was a child, the scent of lavender had always eased her stress and relaxed her. As she began applying the cream to her legs, Loretta walked in.

"Sorry, Ruthie," Loretta started. "I was up and down the ship talking to anyone who might know where the director was, but I couldn't find him."

Ruth sighed. She capped the lotion and set it aside.

Loretta kicked off her shoes just like Ruth had about a half hour ago, and she pulled her pastel scarf from her neck. As she opened the closet next to her and hung the scarf, she continued, "Apparently, this Frederick Scott is a recluse. I spoke to a few people who said he has been locking himself up in his suite ever since he got on the ship, and only comes out when he is needed to work."

"So, the question is, when does he work again?"

Loretta paused and put a finger to the side of her chin, thinking. "I suppose that would have to be when they shoot the season finale. But I'm guessing that might be on hold now that the producer is dead."

"Not necessarily," Ruth said. "I just learned that everything is going as planned."

"Oh?" Loretta scurried over to the bed next to Ruth. She took a seat, facing her friend. "Go on."

"I spoke to Maria."

Loretta's mouth dropped. "No way. *The* Maria Melendez? From *Darkness into Light*? You really talked with her?"

Ruth nodded.

"What did she say?"

"She said the network already forked over a lot of money to reserve the island, and they don't want to take the chance of upsetting their viewers. They have a contract to honor."

"How is she taking Jay's death?"

"That's the thing. She said that she's glad that Hector is taking over."

Loretta scrunched up her forehead. "Hector? Who's that?"

"The co-executive producer. Just like Frederick told John, she said he was writing the script for the shows while Jay got all the credit."

"You're kidding?"

Ruth shook her head.

"That sounds like motive to me."

"Exactly," Ruth said. "But there's more."

"More? Do tell."

Ruth repositioned herself on the bed so that her entire body was facing her friend. "Remember at the meet-and-greet when I had to go to the bathroom?"

"Of course. You almost missed Rafael."

"Well, while I was in there, I heard a woman come in. She was on the phone with someone and said that a man had wronged her, that she was going to finish him."

Loretta's eyes went wide. "No."

"Yes, and she was so angry she threw the phone. It landed near my stall, and I saw that she had cracked the screen. I also saw her shoes. She was wearing canary-yellow stilettos."

"Wait! Isn't that what Maria was wearing during the little show they put on in the atrium?"

"Exactly."

"So, what did you do?"

"Nothing. Until tonight. See, she said that Jay had had a lot of enemies because he had 'wronged them,' which is the same wording she used when she was on the phone—she'd been 'wronged.' But when I asked her how Jay had wronged her, she said he didn't. So, I brought up the conversation she had in the bathroom."

"You didn't!" Loretta shook her head in disbelief. "What did she say?" She inched closer, eager to hear more.

"She said it was none of my business and left."

"Wow. I can't believe it." Loretta stood. "So, we have the director guy, Frederick Scott, who was last seen threatening Jay in the atrium and hasn't come out of his suite. And we have the co-executive producer, Hector, who was writing the scripts for the show, but Jay was taking all the credit…"

"Not to mention, he would be next in line to take on the producer role," Ruth added. "And he probably knew that the network had already paid a pretty penny to get this island and knew the show would go on no matter what, even without Jay."

"Right. And lastly, we have Maria, who might have been betrayed or wronged by Jay in some way and is hiding something."

"And according to Maria, there could be more suspects if Jay was as unlikeable as she claimed he was."

Loretta shook her head. "So that means anyone who is involved with the show and is on the ship. That would include the other actors, Catalina and Gustavo."

"And Rafael," Ruth said, arching an eyebrow.

"You can't possibly think that Rafael, *the* Rafael Javiera, would have anything to do with this?"

"We must keep our options open, which means Rafael should be included in our suspect list."

Loretta looked up at the ceiling as if she were speaking to a higher power. "Please don't let it be Rafael Javiera!"

CHAPTER 10

The next morning, Ruth and Loretta were up bright and early for work. Soon they would be porting at the cruise line's signature private island, Mermaid's Cay. Which meant it would be a busy day in the kitchen working on the mermaid-themed treats for the Mermaid's Dinner, a formal dinner they had on the ship for all the passengers.

As usual, Loretta was whining all morning. It was her least favorite dinner to prep for, but Ruth didn't mind. She loved how they decorated the banquet hall with twinkling white and ocean-blue lights and sashes. And Eric, the ice sculptor, made a different mermaid sculpture each time. Last time, he created an incredible ice sculpture of a mermaid reaching up toward a clam with a pearl. She could only hope this one would be just as breathtaking.

As Ruth was putting on her shoes, Loretta was in the bathroom getting ready and was now singing "Boogie Woogie Bugle Boy," a song she sang often to hype herself up. It was before their time, but it was one song Ruth didn't mind. In fact, she liked the song. It was fun and catchy. Though, Loretta never got the lyrics quite right.

Loretta came out of the bathroom, still humming the tune. "All right. Time to kick some mermaid tail!"

Ruth sighed and shook her head. The day was starting out just like every Mermaid Day, and Ruth knew how it would end. Loretta would get into the kitchen, ready and pumped. Then after a few hours, she would be miserable and complaining about the mermaid-tail cupcakes and how they were too time consuming, and how she was going to find a new job. One that didn't involve another mermaid tail ever again. And by showtime, she would be so frustrated, saying how one day she would tell Janice to shove it up a mermaid's tail.

Ruth and Loretta made their way up to the kitchen, up on deck five. When they walked in, John was already working on the mermaid-tail cupcakes, with a bunch of finished cupcakes behind him.

Both women stepped back in shock. Loretta clutched

her chest. "John?" John wasn't supposed to start work for another few hours, and here he was with almost all of the cupcakes done. The very cupcakes that Loretta always dreaded.

The young man looked up and smiled. "Hey, boss!"

"John, what are you doing?" Ruth asked in the same tone she used when he made a mess. She didn't mean it that way, but that's how it came out.

John's smile faded. "Well, I was up all night at the crew bar, and then I couldn't sleep. It was four in the morning, and I figured, why go to sleep when I could get a head start on the mermaid-tail cupcakes?"

Ruth thought Loretta was going to pass out. But instead, she walked up to John, grabbed him by both shoulders, and stared directly into his eyes. "John," she said.

John looked frightened. "Yeah?"

"You are my hero."

John cocked his head. "Huh?"

To Ruth's surprise, Loretta brought him in and squeezed him. What many people didn't know about Loretta was that she had quite the grip. She wasn't a very strong lady, but she could squeeze the stuffing out of a teddy bear.

John's eyes bulged, and after a few seconds, he attempted to pull away from her, but she held him firm.

John poked her a few times on the shoulder with his free hand. "Uh, Loretta…"

"Hm."

"I can't breathe!" he said between short, exaggerated breaths. The blood vessels in his face looked like they were about to burst.

Loretta held on a bit longer before releasing him. John expelled what sounded like a sharp cough before drawing in more air.

Then she turned to Ruth. "You know what this means?"

Ruth shook her head. John was still behind Loretta, trying to catch his breath. Ruth shrugged.

"We can finally see Mermaid's Cay!"

Loretta was right. Mermaid Day was always so busy that they never got a chance to venture out of the kitchen, let alone the ship, and explore the island. Ruth had heard so many great things about it. Her heart started beating harder in excitement.

"You can come too, John," Ruth said over Loretta's shoulder. The redness in his face was beginning to fade back to his natural color as he sucked in more oxygen. He was bent over, hands over his knees. He brought one hand up and gave her a quick wave.

Loretta smiled. "It's settled, then. All we have to do is get the rest of the cakes done, and we are free! Let's go,

John!" She grabbed John by the apron. A little "whoa" escaped him as she pulled him to the frosting station. "You can help me with the buttercream icing."

Ruth let out a chuckle. Little did John know, he was now Loretta's best friend.

Later that day, they were finished with all the prepping, and with Janice's permission, John, Loretta, and Ruth were making their way up through the atrium to get off the ship. They had to be back a couple of hours before the passengers to work on the layout and presentation. And Ruth would be in charge of helping the waitstaff with the desserts as well. It didn't leave them with a lot of time, but Ruth wasn't complaining. She was just happy to finally see the island.

She had her bag with her, and double-checked that she'd brought sunscreen and a novel. Dressed in her bathing suit and coverup, she also wore a sun hat and her white-rimmed sunglasses. Loretta was in a similar getup, while John had his flamingo trunks on, a white tee, and flip-flops.

As they were getting off the ship, Gerald greeted them. He was part of the staff and always looked sharp. Though, in Ruth's opinion, he wore a little too much hair gel, which left his hair looking wet and slick all the time. But he always combed it in such a way that he looked rather dashing. He smiled as she approached, showing off his dimples.

"Surprised to see you three today," he said. "They not giving you enough work to do on Mermaid Day?"

Loretta pulled John toward her. "This guy is our savior. He's the one who made it possible for us to finally see Mermaid's Cay."

"John?" Gerald let out a chuckle. "Must have done something right if Loretta is this happy on Mermaid Day."

Ruth laughed. "That's for sure. All it took was baking and decorating hundreds of mermaid-tail cupcakes."

Gerald paused. "Wow. All by yourself?"

John nodded. "It was easier than it sounds. I batched them."

"I don't care what you did," Loretta said. "I'm just so glad you did."

"Well, don't let me keep you." Gerald stepped aside to let them pass. Then he said, "Oh, I almost forgot. The east side is off limits."

Ruth's shoulders dropped. Though she didn't know if she was even interested in the east side of Mermaid's Cay, she would have liked to see it to make that decision. "Why?"

"That show, *Darkness into Light*, is shooting over there."

Loretta's eyes went wide. "Oh, yeah, that's right. I almost forgot!"

Ruth placed her hands on her hips and arched an eyebrow. "Really?"

"Yes, really," Loretta said, folding her arms across her chest. "What are you trying to say?"

"Nothing. It just explains why you were extra grumpy about the mermaid tails."

"I'm always grumpy about the mermaid tails. I don't see what that has to do with anything?"

Gerald and John stood there, their eyes darting back and forth between the two women.

Finally, Gerald interrupted, "Ladies, ladies. Let's not spoil a beautiful day like this, eh?"

"Gerald's right," Loretta said, tipping her chin upward, ready to head down the gangway.

"One thing before you go," Gerald said.

Loretta paused. "What?"

"That area is closed off, and I was directed to let everyone know to please stay away from the set. Trespassers will be escorted back to the ship."

"I wouldn't dream of trespassing anywhere," Loretta said.

"Aren't the passengers upset that they can't go to that area?" Ruth asked.

Gerald shook his head. "It's away from all the bars, and there's plenty of the beach free for them to use."

Ruth nodded. "Well, thanks, Gerald."

Gerald smiled. "Enjoy your time."

As they walked out onto the island, Loretta said, "Oh, isn't this the best day ever?"

"Sure is." Ruth looked around. "Can't wait to get a sangria and find a nice spot on the beach."

John pointed to a stand. "Oh, look! Snorkeling!"

Loretta grabbed him by the elbow. "No, *Darkness into Light* will be shooting here. We got to check that out."

John furrowed his eyebrows. "But Gerald just said—"

"Gerald, Shmarald," Loretta said, batting the air with her hand. "I'm going to check it out."

"No, Loretta," John said. "We could get in trouble. Right, Ruth?" He eyed Ruth expectantly. She didn't know what to say. On one hand, she just wanted to grab a fruity drink—maybe a coconut one, too—and relax on the beach with some sunscreen and a good book. But on the other, she really wanted to get to the bottom of the mystery. Nothing excited her more, and there was a victim, which meant there was a killer running around the ship. There was only one thing to do.

Ruth puffed up her chest and lifted her chin.

"Trouble is my middle name," Ruth said, looking out into the horizon.

John lightly cleared his throat. "I thought 'Marie' was your middle name."

Ruth let out a breath. "It's an expression, John."

"Right," he said. "So, I guess that means…"

Loretta shouted, "Off we go to the *Darkness into Light* set!"

CHAPTER 11

Ruth wished she hadn't brought along her beach bag. If she would have known they were going to stalk the members and crew of *Darkness into Light* at their set, she would never have lugged it along. She had recently bought it at one of the promenade shops on the ship, and it was her favorite. It caught her eye from the shop's window as she was walking by one day, probably on her way to track down Loretta so she wouldn't go bankrupt at the ship's casino. Ruth could've sworn that not only was there a glow that haloed around the bag, but that she heard angels singing. It had called to her. What could she do? Though it was canvas, it was a nautical black and white striped bag that was lined with blonde leather stitched around the corners and covering the straps. It was not only stylish, able to be worn even on non-beach days where no one would bat an eye, but it also matched everything.

They tiptoed around the back, where some sort of partitions were set up, likely the walls used for the show's set. As they approached a corner, Loretta put a finger to her lips, signaling to keep quiet before they rounded the corner. But as they did, they ran into another person sneaking around the other way. They all let out a little yelp before Ruth recognized who it was.

"Wanda? What are you doing here?" Ruth asked.

Wanda touched her red hair with her palm as if she were making sure it was still there and in place. Though, a hurricane could have come through at that very moment and it wouldn't have moved an inch with the amount of hairspray she put in it. In fact, if Gerald wasn't almost three decades younger, they'd probably make a good couple. "I got some time off from the salon," she said. "What are you all doing here?"

Loretta put her hands on her hips. "We got time off too."

Wanda tilted her head to the side, confused. "From the kitchen?"

All three of them—Ruth, Loretta, and John—nodded in unison.

"On Mermaid Day?"

They all nodded again.

Finally, Ruth spoke up: "What were you doing, anyway, Wanda?"

"Nothing, just trying to find a good spot to take a peek at what's going on on the set."

Loretta shook her head. "You're trying to see Rafael."

"Of course, I'm trying to see Rafael. Aren't you?"

Loretta backed down.

Ruth stepped up. "Actually, we are trying to see if we can find any more clues on who could've had a motive to kill Jay."

"Me too." Wanda eyed all of them one by one. "We should check it out together."

"I don't know," Loretta said. "Three is already a crowd."

Wanda shrugged. "Well, we'll leave John."

Just then, someone hurried around the corner, wearing a headset with a microphone. "What is going on here? Who are you all?" Ruth only hoped the microphone by their lips was turned off.

John tensed. "Well, I guess I'll be checking out the snorkeling now," he said as he backed up a few steps, then turned around and fled.

Scaredy cat, Ruth thought, though the other two women were probably thinking the same thing.

"This is a closed set." The man looked behind them, checking to see if anyone was coming. He turned back to the women. "You better go before someone sees you. They will escort you right on out of here if you're caught."

"Of course," Ruth said. "We just got lost. We'll be on our way now."

All three women turned and walked away in the same direction John had gone, walking until they reached a palm tree. Ruth looked back just in time to see the man with the headset disappear back behind the wall for the set.

The women formed a huddle behind the palm tree.

Loretta gave Wanda a sideways glance. "I told you three's a crowd."

Wanda shrugged. "So, what do we do now?"

"I say we split up," Ruth said. "It's obvious we can't get too close to the set, but there are a lot of people just standing around. We just have to look like we belong. You know, act confident, and maybe one of us can find information."

"Look like we belong? We both look like a couple of beach bums in our bathing suits and coverups," Loretta said, pointing to herself and Ruth. "It'll never work."

"Actually—" Wanda started.

"They said we can't be near the set," Ruth interrupted. "I'm sure we can get away with walking around it."

"No, that's what Headset Guy said," Loretta argued. "Gerald said this whole area is closed."

Wanda tried again. "Well, if I could just…"

Ruth shook her head. "Who are you going to listen to, the guy on the set or 'greasy hair' Gerald?"

"Girls!" Wanda said.

Both women jumped, eyes wide. They looked at Wanda.

Wanda continued, voice lower and gentler, "I think I may know a way to fix our little problem." She tugged on the huge bag she always carried with her and began digging. She pulled out a pair of pants and a pair of capris. "I have tops, too, if you need them."

Ruth and Loretta gave her a confused look.

"Why in the world would you be carrying extra sets of clothing?" Loretta asked.

"The question isn't why would I carry extra sets of clothes. The question is why don't *you* carry extra sets of clothes?"

Loretta furrowed her eyebrows.

Wanda continued, "I always carry extra sets of clothing because you never know when you'll need them."

"Like, for a sting operation?"

Wanda dropped her shoulders, rolling her eyes. "No," she said. "I mean if the weather changes and you get cold, or if you spill something on your top or—" Wanda lowered her voice. "In case you have a little accident." She pointed downward toward her pants.

Loretta nodded slightly. "Hm, never thought of that." She turned to Ruth. "She has a point, and it's a pretty good idea."

"Well," Wanda said, holding out the pants. "Take your pick."

Ruth grabbed the white capris while Loretta took the blue pants. Ruth opened the capris and held them up, eyeing the size. "I think they're a little big for me."

Wanda shot Ruth a look that could kill.

Ruth held the pants to her waist. "I'm just saying."

Wanda huffed and dug in her bag some more. She pulled out a belt and handed it to Ruth. "Here, use this."

Loretta looked at the tag inside her pants and was clearly taken aback by what she saw. "Wanda, are you really this size?" She was clearly suspicious in her tone.

Wanda jabbed both of her fists into her hips. "What are you insinuating, Loretta?"

Loretta shrugged. "Nothing. I'm just observant, that's all." She shook the pants and stepped into them. They seemed to fit Loretta just right. Then Loretta dug into her own bag and pulled out a tube of lipstick and applied it. It was a darker shade, a nice contrast to her porcelain complexion. She already looked like she could fit in with the many people standing around the set with her sunglasses, lipstick, scarf, and pants.

Loretta handed Ruth the lipstick as she was finishing slipping the end of the belt into the last loop in the capris. The capris were a little baggy in the thighs and rear, but the belt certainly helped. Ruth took the lipstick and smoothed it over her lips, then made a pop sound after she was done blending it. "How do I look?" she asked, adjusting her hat.

Wanda and Loretta analyzed her and then looked at each other, shaking their heads.

"What?" Ruth asked.

"The capris and belt look a little silly with your bathing suit top," Wanda said.

Ruth looked at herself. Wanda was right. She looked ridiculous with her loose white capri pants over her fluorescent, polka-dot bathing suit. She didn't match.

Wanda pulled out a sleeveless red top. "Here. Put this on."

Ruth slipped the top over her head and adjusted it. She put her arms out. "Now how do I look?"

Both women nodded. "Good" and "perfect" were the words they used to describe her.

"Great," Ruth said. "Now, Wanda, you take the left side of the set. Loretta, you get the right, and I'll take the back. We'll all meet here at the palm tree in an hour."

All the women nodded and dispersed, setting off on their mission.

CHAPTER 12

Ruth cut around to the back of the set. When she got closer to one of the makeshift walls, she aligned herself against it. The murmurs of maybe a hundred or so people could be heard from behind that wall. She adjusted her shades so that they sat up the bridge of her nose, closer to her eyes to hide her identity better, before slipping around the corner.

She took a deep breath; her nerves were starting to get the best of her. It wasn't like she was going to be on the set, in front of the many people working there, watching her. Or worse, filmed and put on air for millions to watch on TV and the internet. But she was about to go into an area that was restricted, not only for the average vacationer but for her too. Actually, even more so for her. If caught, she could not only land herself in a heap of trouble, but she could lose her job.

Had she forgotten that this was her plan? What was she thinking? The butterflies in her stomach were now making their way up to her chest, fluttering chaotically. If she wasn't careful, one might make its way all the way up. She swallowed it down.

Now or never.

She pushed herself off the wall and rounded the corner to the other side in confident strides. There was the hustle and bustle of people with walkie-talkies, carrying lights, boom mics, and clipboards. Some of the people were directing others where to go and where to set up. It would've been more intimidating with the many people rushing, moving things, and ordering others, but they were so focused on their own duties that they hadn't even seemed to notice Ruth enter.

She looked to her right. There was a small group of people standing by a large mirror. A woman, with brushes and a range of skin-tone colors next to her on a table, flipped a brush over one of the pallets and dusted the powder over the forehead and nose of a man. Ruth could only see the side profile of the guy sitting in the chair in front of her.

Another man came around one of the corners from

what Ruth could only imagine would be the set and said, "Gustavo, you're on in ten!"

Gustavo gave the man a thumbs up. Then he asked the woman, still frantically powdering his nose, if she was almost done.

"If you would stop sweating," she replied.

"Can't help it." He gave the front of his shirt several tugs to cool himself down.

"It's hot on this island."

Just then, Ruth could hear the clomping of a set of stilettos coming. She looked in the direction from which she heard the footsteps to see a tall, beautiful woman, her long, curled locks bouncing as she walked. It was Maria Melendez. Ruth pulled the brim of her black-and-white hat down and turned away. If anyone would recognize her, it would be Maria. On the table next to Ruth was a folder with papers. She picked it up and began leafing through it as if she were busy and belonged there.

When the clicking of her heels faded in the distance, Ruth turned back around to see Gustavo. The makeup artist was gone, and she'd been replaced by a blonde actress. It took a moment before Ruth remembered what character this woman played—Catalina.

"Have you heard from them yet?" Gustavo asked her.

The blonde woman shook her head. "I left them a

voicemail and…" She gave a shrug and dropped her hands to her sides. "I just can't believe it…my big opportunity, and I just let it slip through my fingers."

"Don't worry. It could be nothing. Everything has been crazy since Jay's accident."

Catalina looked at the ground.

Gustavo continued, "You worked hard for this. And look, now you are an actress on one of the most popular shows on Earth. This *is* your big break. You've made it!"

Catalina gave a weak smile. Then she moved in closer to him, wrapping her arms around him in a friendly hug. He reciprocated, and after a moment in their embrace, he pulled away and grabbed her by the shoulder, looking into her eyes. "You're already a superstar."

If Ruth didn't know any better, she'd think that they were acting out a scene right in front of her.

"Actually," Catalina said, "we all know the beautiful Maria Melendez is the real superstar," she said, saying her name in a thick Spanish accent.

"Nah, that's not true. You are the, how you say…" he paused, thinking a moment. Then his eyes lit up in realization, as if the words had just hit him. "The blonde bombshell."

Catalina laughed. "You always know the right thing to say."

They were a nice pair. Genuine and supportive. A far cry from what she'd imagine from a couple of stars in a hit telenovela show. The only person she didn't see was the man who played the big star, Romeo—Rafael Javiera. And just as if he'd heard his cue, Rafael came around a corner on the far end, behind Gustavo and Catalina. He walked briskly toward them.

"Hey! Good afternoon, my friends," he said, his smile beaming so bright, Ruth almost had to squint her eyes behind her sunglasses. He shook Gustavo's hand and then turned to Catalina, taking her hand and patting it with his other hand. They all seemed happy.

A voice called out from behind her. "I need Gustavo and Catalina on set, please!"

Ruth turned toward the voice, still with the folder in her hand. There were two men standing there, waiting. Ruth recognized the director from the meet-and-greet. The one who'd been arguing with Jay, and threatened him the night of his death: Frederick Scott.

Gustavo and Catalina regarded Rafael with a nod and wave as they made their way to the set.

Ruth moved closer to where Frederick Scott was talking to another fellow. She took the folder of papers with her, pretending to study what was inside. As she slowly walked past, she could hear Frederick Scott say, "Make sure Gustavo and Catalina are facing opposite directions. I want Cameras A and B on him and Cameras C and D on her, so we can get the angle I was telling you about."

The man nodded, taking note.

The director continued, "Now, with Jay gone, I can finally direct the season finale how it should be done."

Ruth stopped, focused on keeping herself from gasping out loud. What had she just heard?

The man nodded again, and briskly walked away toward the set, seemingly unaware of what the director had just said. Could that man really be this oblivious? The director was about to follow the man's lead, when there was a beeping sound coming from his pants. He rummaged in his pocket and pulled out his cell phone, checking the screen. He let out a frustrated breath and swiped his thumb to the right, putting the phone to his ear.

"Yes, Hector," Frederick Scott said. It was clear by his tone he was irritated. "Yes, I know. I'm on it." Ending the call, he shoved the phone back into his pocket. He threw his hands up in the air and said out loud to no one in particular, "The guy has been executive producer for five minutes, and he's already getting on my last nerve. Maybe he should throw *himself* overboard next."

Ruth's eyes went wide. Now she knew she was hearing things. How could this man say these horrible things loud enough for anyone to hear? She watched as Frederick Scott made his way to the set, rounding the corner where Gustavo and Catalina had gone. Ruth craned her neck to the left and then to the right. Though there were still a lot of people around, the area had cleared out quite a bit. Everyone had most likely made their way to the set themselves to continue their work or to watch the scene they were shooting.

Ruth glanced at her watch. She still had some time. So, the question was, should she find Loretta and Wanda before one of them got caught or should she snoop just a little bit more?

CHAPTER 13

Ruth had been walking around behind the set for a while. The director, Frederick Scott, had yelled out, "Cut!" and "Action!" periodically between the actors' dramatic lines. Only Gustavo and Catalina could be heard on the set, in what sounded like a heated argument. Ruth tried listening in on any of the employees lingering around about the actors, or to determine if there were any suspicions regarding Jay Juan's death. But instead, she only caught bits and pieces of people unleashing horror stories about the guy.

Apparently, he'd had his hands in everything when it came to the show. The casting, the schedule, and the negotiations. Some even knew about the gash on his head. The makeup artist said that he had made a pass at her, but she ignored him. It was clear that the woman had been worried about her job, though, since she'd heard that Jay had made passes at another employee, and when she had refused, she was fired for some made-up reason. Ruth shook her head. Though the stories she was hearing were terrible, and she'd hope that they weren't true, upon further listening, she didn't sense that any of the employees confessing their experiences with Jay were real suspects to his death.

It had been an hour, and Ruth made her way back to the palm tree to meet Loretta and Wanda. They were talking amongst themselves as Ruth approached.

"Did you see Romeo when he walked in on Gustavo and Catalina in that embrace?" she could hear Loretta asking Wanda.

"Their rendezvous is finally up," Wanda said. "I knew the whole time."

"You did not."

"I did so. It would only make sense, if Romeo and Maria are having an affair, that his wife and her fiancé would also be meeting in secret. It's the basic telenovela formula."

Loretta scoffed at her.

"Did either of you do any investigating?" Ruth asked, looking at them both. "Or were you both too busy watching the story?"

Wanda jabbed her fists into her hips. "I'll have you know that I did do some investigating."

"And?"

Wanda broke eye contact, redirecting her gaze to her feet. "I didn't find anything."

"What about you, Loretta?" Ruth asked.

"I learned that the pastries they're having today on the buffet table were flown in by Blue Box Foods."

"What does that have to do with Jay's murder?" Ruth asked, confused.

"Nothing." Loretta shrugged. "I'm just offended. Why didn't they have us bake them? Don't they like our pastries?"

Wanda rolled her eyes.

"I think we should consider ourselves lucky," Ruth said. "If they did, we'd be stuck in the kitchen right now, baking more than just mermaid-tail cupcakes."

"True," Loretta said in agreement. "So, did you learn anything?"

"Yes. But let's go to the sandbar over there to talk." Ruth pointed to the outside bar that was closer to the beach, away from the bustle of the set.

Wanda clapped her hands in excitement. "Oh, yes, let's!" She turned. "I need a drink." She tottered ahead of her friends, making a direct route to the bar.

Heat radiated from the sand as layers of it drifted over Ruth's toes through her sandals as she walked. When they approached the bar, Ruth took a stool between Wanda and Loretta. Before they could even order their drinks, John came clomping in long strides, still wearing flippers. He had goggles with a snorkel tube attached to them atop his head and a wide grin stretched across his face. It was quite a sight with his white-and-pink flamingo swimming trunks and lobster-colored skin, and for the final touch, a thick layer of white sunblock on his nose.

"Oh dear," Loretta said, slowly shaking her head, eyes locked on the sight of John approaching. "And I was beginning to have high hopes for the kid."

Ruth nudged her.

John continued his clumsy march to the bar right up next to Loretta, but he didn't engage with her. Instead, he yelled, "Hey, Sammy!" He held up an empty glass with a half-eaten celery stick for the bartender to see and said, "Another Virgin Mary, please!" John regarded the three of them and smiled. "Hey, my favorite women are back." He gave them all a wink. "Learn anything new about Jay Juan?"

"You'd know if you didn't bail on us," Wanda said. "Wimp."

John frowned. "They said we weren't allowed near the set."

Loretta looked John up and down. "Well, I see you found something else to keep yourself occupied."

John's bright smile returned. "Yeah, snorkeling. You should try it. You can come with me, Loretta. I'm looking for a partner."

Loretta shook her head. "No way. Give me an alcoholic drink and a chair and I'm happy."

John shrugged. "Suit yourself." The bartender appeared with a fresh drink for John. "I bid you adieu," John said to the three women. And with that, he shimmied himself away from the bar so he could turn himself around. He took a quick sip of his drink, gave a curt nod, and began making his complicated trek back to the water.

All three women shook their heads simultaneously.

"Something's clearly wrong with that child," Wanda said, still watching him make his journey.

"So, ladies," the bartender said. "What would you like?"

Loretta and Wanda each ordered a martini, while Ruth opted for a sangria. No one could make her a martini quite as good as her buddy Geoff, so the sangria would have to suffice. When he returned with their drinks, Ruth took a sip. It wasn't bad. Not bad at all. She took another sip of her fruity drink.

"Okay, girls," Ruth said. "Back to business."

"Yes." Loretta placed her martini down gently on the bar. "What did you find out?"

"So," Ruth said. "I think we need to dig a little more into the director, Frederick Scott."

Wanda's eyes went wide. "Oh, I heard from one of the staff workers on the set that he's tough to work with. A snob, they call him."

"I don't blame them," Loretta started. "That guy reminds me of my ex-husband, Barry. That snake."

Wanda furrowed her eyebrows. "He doesn't look anything like Barry."

Wanda was right. From how Loretta had described the man, Barry was bald, with caterpillar eyebrows, and straggly nose hairs that matched the silver strands growing from his ears. And not to mention the beer belly that hung over his belt. The director, Frederick Scott, on the other hand, was so thin the popular skinny jeans would be loose on him. He seemed to always be clomping around in boots and had a dark yet petite goatee. And, of course, was decades younger.

"I didn't say he looked like Barry," Loretta argued. "I said he reminds me of him." Then Loretta let out a huff and mumbled under her breath something about if only she had known how much of a snake he was, she'd have never married the slimy, no-good little gremlin.

Once she got started on her ex-husband, she had a

hard time letting it go. Usually, Ruth could calm her down by bringing up Loretta's high school sweetheart and long-time husband, Ernie, who had died almost a decade ago unexpectedly. From the stories Loretta had told her, it wasn't until she found Barry, aka "the snake" as Loretta liked to call him, that she began to smile again. They'd gotten hitched after only four months of seeing each other. The marriage only lasted a few years before divorce came down like a sledgehammer. It was swift and quick.

"I think we should also look into Maria," Wanda said, ignoring Loretta's grumbling.

"I do have my suspicions of her," Ruth said. "I heard her on the phone in the bathroom the night of the meet-and-greet."

"Oh?"

"I don't know who she was talking to, but she said that someone had done her wrong for the last time, and she made a threat toward them. Then I crossed paths with her at Geoff's bar."

Loretta chimed in, "What she means is that she 'crossed paths' with her," Loretta said, using quotation fingers as she said the words.

"Okay, so I kind of planned to bump into her there," Ruth corrected herself. "I talked to her, and she said that producer Jay Juan *wronged* many people."

Wanda put her drink down. "Interesting choice of words. Did you say anything?"

Ruth nodded. "Of course, I did. I had to."

"Really?"

"Yes. After I downed my drink, I asked her about the phone conversation in the bathroom. I asked her how he wronged her."

"What did she say?"

Ruth shook her head. "She said it was none of my business and got up and walked away."

"Guilty!" Wanda shouted.

Ruth shook her head. "We can't jump to conclusions like that."

"Why not? She basically confessed."

"Hardly."

"I know it's her!" Wanda said.

"But I haven't told you what I overheard Frederick Scott say."

Both Loretta and Wanda leaned in, waiting. Wanda winded her hand, the signal to hurry up. "Well..."

"I heard him say that now that Jay is gone, he can finally direct the show as it should be done."

Loretta and Wanda glanced at each other, eyes wide. "Motive?" Loretta asked.

"Possibly. But there's more."

"Well, tell us already," Wanda said impatiently.

"Hector, the co-executive producer, called him, and when he got off the phone with him, he said that the man was already getting on his last nerve, and that he should throw himself overboard next."

Both women gasped, their eyes the size of saucers.

"No!" Loretta said.

Ruth nodded.

"So, now what's the plan?" Wanda asked.

"Now Loretta and I will go back in the kitchen and finish prepping for the Mermaid Dinner. The stars will most likely be there, with it being a formal dinner and all."

"And the biggest dinner," Wanda said.

Ruth pointed at her red-headed friend. "Exactly. Loretta and I will do our rounds like we always do, helping the waitstaff and talking to the guests about their experience with us, and we'll see if we can learn any more information."

"What should I do?" Wanda asked.

"Nothing. It will be too suspicious if you're there. We'll meet you in the lobby outside the banquet hall."

Wanda crossed her arms. "That doesn't sound very exciting."

"No. But I don't think Janice will appreciate you crashing the formal dinner."

Loretta nodded. "Janice will probably be suspicious

anyway. She's always stressed out during Mermaid's Dinner."

"All right, all right," Wanda said. She downed the rest of her drink. Placing the glass down on the bar, she added, "I'll wait outside in the lobby."

Ruth smiled. "Great. Let's go."

They all hopped off their stools and began their trek back to the ship.

Wanda said, "By the way, I want my clothes back. I'm not running a charity, you know." She pointed at the blouse and pants Ruth wore. "And they'd better be cleaned and pressed, too!"

CHAPTER 14

Back in the kitchen, Ruth and Loretta were adding the final touches to a five-layer cake with a silky meringue buttercream frosting, while John finished decorating the sea-salt caramel cupcakes—a highly popular treat during Mermaid's Dinner and other formal banquets aboard the *Splendor of the Seas*. The five-layer cake, however, was the centerpiece of the desserts—besides the mermaid ice sculpture, of course. Each tier was made up of a white almond sour cream cake. Ruth had picked this particular type of cake for several reasons. First, because it was familiar to most people as the traditional wedding cake taste, which people often equated to a big celebration. Second, it was simple, and she liked simple on these most hectic days.

As for the sea-salt caramel cupcakes, John had

argued that they should add a pretzel topping, but Ruth had shot down his idea. She was worried about the texture and that it was against the recipe approved by Janice.

"What if we use thin pretzels and chop them in a food processor and then sprinkle it on top?" John asked.

Ruth shook her head. "It'll still have a dry texture on top of the silky, smooth caramel frosting." She understood and appreciated John's eagerness and enthusiasm to create. She too had that drive to always try to make a recipe even better, but there were rules they had to abide by, and they didn't have the time to experiment now. All recipes and recipe changes had to be run by Janice, and there was no way she was going to approve anything new this close to Mermaid's Dinner. "I think it's best if you just stick to the recipe, John. Add the flaky sea salt on top as decoration. And make sure you use the Maldon."

"All right, all right," John said, surrendering in defeat.

Ruth tried the frosting John had been whipping up for the cupcakes. Her eyes went wide. "My, John, this is better than my own!"

John smiled. "I added more dark brown sugar and extra butter. I also whipped the butter and the sugar at a lower heat."

"This is fantastic," she said, enjoying another taste.

"Let me try it," Loretta said, grabbing a clean spoon. She dipped it into the frosting. "Oh, boy. Yes. When I didn't think this cupcake could get any better."

Ruth pointed to the open notebook in front of John. "Change it in our recipe binder." John smiled and grabbed a pencil. Okay, so there were times Ruth secretly overrode Janice's approval, but it was only when it was absolutely necessary.

"And don't do that again, John," Ruth said.

The smile disappeared on John's face.

"You need to run these changes by me first," she said, though she couldn't help but enjoy yet another taste of the icing.

Loretta shifted her weight, jutting out her hip to one side. "Hey, don't hog it!"

"I need that for the cupcakes, Ruth," John said, his smile slowly returning.

"I know, I know. Just making sure it's good enough for the guests."

"I think we've established that it's more than good," Loretta said, taking the spoon from Ruth.

"Okay, so all we have to do is add the final touches to all the cakes, and we can start bringing them out to the dining hall." Ruth pointed to Loretta. "You finish piping the five-layer cake, and I'll help John finish salting the cupcakes."

Everyone began scrambling. Ruth had to admit, trying to beat the clock decorating a massive cake and hundreds of cupcakes, and not to mention the other desserts the other bakers she supervised were creating, then presenting them all was a rush, and she loved it. It made her feel alive, and she was always up for the challenge.

As they were running around, bringing cakes out into the banquet hall and arranging them on the tables, Janice walked over in long strides, holding her clipboard. She started making what looked like tick marks on her paper as she eyeballed the tables and displays. "Where are the mermaid tails?" she asked.

Ruth knew she was forgetting something. "We still have them in the back."

"They're no good in the back. I need them front and center on a table on the other side of the five-layer cake." Janice looked at her watch and let out a sharp breath. "We have five minutes to get them out here on display."

Ruth rushed back into the kitchen, grabbing Loretta on the way. "Where's John?"

"I think he's still in the kitchen."

When they hurried back there, they found John pulling out the mermaid tails from the back. He turned to them as he was carrying a large tray of the cupcakes. "Almost forgot about these."

Ruth sighed, realizing she was out of breath. "John, you are a life saver. We need to get these out pronto! Janice is pitching a fit already. We've got five minutes."

"No worries, boss. I'm on it," he said with a big grin. "I'll pull more from the back if you and Loretta want to take them out."

Ruth nodded, taking the first set of cupcakes out to the table. She wasn't sure how she was going to fit them all out there. Though, this was a thought she'd had many times before. They always figured it out.

When they finished getting all the cakes out for display, Janice went through her checklist again. Ruth held her breath, hoping she hadn't forgotten anything else. "Looks like everything's accounted for," Janice said, looking up from her clipboard. "Great job, everyone."

Ruth let out a much-needed exhale. She took off her apron and went to the bathroom to cleanup, combing her fingers through her hair and applying a new swipe of lipstick. It was showtime.

In only moments, they opened the large, double mahogany doors, and people shuffled in. They were well dressed in suits, and some in tuxedos complete with bowties, while the women were dressed in beautiful gowns and glittering jewelry, clutches, and glamorous shoes. Ruth and Loretta stood by their displays, talking with the guests. They always wanted to know how she and Loretta were able to bake such beautiful cakes.

As Ruth was talking to a couple from Long Beach, she heard a *psst* sound coming from behind her. She turned around to see Loretta standing there.

Loretta whispered, "Look who just walked in." She pointed to the strapping young man. The star of *Darkness into Light*, Rafael Javiera, aka Romeo, had entered the room alongside a big man with dark sunglasses and an expressionless face—a bodyguard, perhaps? Romeo was in a dark suit, with wingtip shoes and no tie. His smile was just as bright as the white shirt under his jacket. He was shaking hands with one of the greeters at the door while a small group of people formed around him.

Ruth had a hard time tearing her eyes from the dashing actor. "I have to say, the man is stunning."

"Sharp dresser, too," Loretta added.

"Wonder where the rest of the actors are?"

"Maybe they're not coming. They're probably having exclusive parties in their massive suites." When Ruth said massive, she meant it. The royal suites were lofts with two floors, a bar, a king-sized bed with a Duxiana mattress, a big-screen TV, and even a mini grand piano, complete with modern art and a balcony at least as big as the loft itself.

"Should we go talk to him?" Loretta asked.

"No, not yet. We'll wait until he's settled. We don't want to seem eager."

"Good idea."

Ruth returned to the guests who were sampling her desserts. As she was finishing up a conversation about Mardi Gras King Cakes with a beautiful woman from Louisiana, Romeo approached, eyeing the caramel cupcakes.

"Good evening," Romeo said, shaking her hand. "Ruth, is it?"

"Yes, how did you remember?"

"How could I ever forget the most beautiful woman I've ever seen?"

Warmth radiated from Ruth's cheeks, and she took a quick breath to steady herself. Of course, the man was clearly lying—she was old enough to be his grandmother. "No, really?"

Romeo chuckled. "You are good. You see right through me, my friend." Then he pointed to John, who wore an impish grin and was giving her a thumbs-up. Perhaps the young baker had put Romeo up to this?

Ruth shook her head in embarrassment.

"Your friend over there reminded me of your name,"

Romeo said. "I do meet a lot of people in a day, but I do remember you. I told you I would stop by to try your desserts."

Ruth put her hands on her hips and narrowed her eyes at him, suspiciously. "So, are you saying you came down to Mermaid's Dinner just to see me?"

"Well, of course, and for the lobster tail they'll be serving. I could never turn that down."

Ruth laughed. "I guess I wouldn't either." She had to admit, the man was a charmer.

"So, what is this little cake?"

"Those are the caramel cupcakes with a light sprinkle of sea salt on top. It's one of our top desserts."

"Oh, a fan favorite. I must try it, then." He picked one of the cupcakes up and began undressing it.

"Would you like a plate?" Ruth asked.

"That won't be necessary." He took a big bite out of the cake, furrowing his eyebrows as he chewed. He swallowed and said, "Wow, this is delicious. I see why it's considered your best. You wouldn't think so, though. It's not as magnificent looking as, say, your five-layer cake over there."

Ruth smiled. "We put a lot of time and thought into these little cakes." Now it was time for her to dig into the drama of *Darkness into Light*. "So, how is everything going with the show?"

Romeo shrugged. "I thought Jay's death was going to be a massive setback. It was certainly a hard hit, but I think Hector will do fine. He learned a lot working with Jay, and he has Frederick, the director, to help him too. Frederick's been around the block quite a bit in the business, so he really knows his stuff." Romeo took another copious bite of his cupcake, leaving him with only one small bite left.

"I heard Frederick is hard to work with. Is that true?"

Romeo took a moment, chewing longer than necessary. Ruth was beginning to think he was stalling. "I wouldn't say that. Sure, he can be a little rough around the edges, but he's a great director. He's always been good to me, and I've never seen him being difficult with anyone."

"What about with Jay? I'm sure they butt heads once in a while."

"Producers and directors do sometimes." Romeo popped the last cupcake morsel into his mouth, then moved to stand next to Ruth. "Frederick is an artist." He put his hands up, creating a square, mimicking a TV or a movie being shot. Both Ruth and Romeo looked through his imaginary camera, groups of people walking in and out of his frame. "He has a vision, and he likes to make those visions come to life on the screen." He dropped his hands and turned toward Ruth, facing her. "And then there's Jay, the producer, who is more realistic and rational. He only sees numbers, dollar amounts, and time. So yes, they had their arguments. But if you're insinuating that Frederick Scott had something to do with Jay's death—" Romeo paused, shaking his head in disapproval at the mere thought of anyone having such an inkling. "Frederick wouldn't hurt a fly. He's vegetarian, you know. It literally sickens him to see a person eat any animal or fish. So, no, he's not a killer."

Ruth nodded. "I understand."

"Well, it was nice talking to you, Ruth. If you don't mind, I would like to try that five-layer cake with the buttercream frosting." He pointed to the cake towering over another collection of colorful cupcakes, also with buttercream frosting. "It's been singing to me since I laid eyes upon it when I walked in." He gave Ruth a gentle pat on her shoulder and made his way to the extravagant cake.

Within seconds, Loretta rushed over. "What did he say?"

Ruth dropped her hands by her sides. "He said Frederick isn't the killer."

"How does he know?"

Ruth didn't look at her friend. She was too busy watching Romeo as he held his plate of cake and grabbed a fork. She shrugged. "Apparently, Frederick is a vegetarian."

Romeo turned to Ruth and gave her a quick salute with the fork before heading back to his table.

Loretta followed Ruth's gaze to Romeo. Then she furrowed her eyebrows. "A vegetarian?"

CHAPTER 15

Ruth walked behind Loretta to their cabin as her roommate rummaged in her bag for the keycard. After the formal dinner came to a close, they had gone to the lobby right outside the Mermaid's Dinner Room to look for Wanda, but she wasn't there. They had both hurried to the casino, a prime Wanda hotspot, when they ran into Betty, who told them she was at Bingo. This was odd to both Ruth and Loretta, but they went to the room that held Bingo nights almost every evening anyway. And lo and behold, to their surprise, there was Wanda. Apparently, she had run into a man who she described as a stud muffin—a dreamboat. To her defense, he was a very good-looking man—square chin, broad shoulders, snow-white hair, a deep baritone voice, and crystal-blue eyes.

This wasn't uncommon for Wanda, as she was a divorcée and often held a brief relationship that only lasted the duration of the trip. Ruth was just surprised she hadn't found the man sooner. Usually, Wanda was a magnet to these men. She could sniff them out like a hound. Though, Ruth imagined it was all the excitement of the *Darkness into Light* stars that had covered their scent.

This time, Wanda claimed to have been so entranced by his cologne that she had followed it all the way to Bingo. Ruth reminded Wanda that she didn't even like Bingo, but Wanda was too busy staring at her new love interest and waved them away. Who were they to stand in the way of a friend's moonstruck obsession? Maybe there were some things more important than *Darkness into Light*, after all.

When they entered their cabin, Loretta made a beeline for the bathroom, as she always did after a long day in the kitchen and dining hall. Ruth walked over to her bed and plopped down, kicking off her shoes, and let out a small groan of relief to finally be off her feet. She watched as Loretta took off her earrings in front of the mirror. She was too tired to do anything else, for the moment.

"So, what does Frederick Scott being a vegetarian

have to do with whether or not he could kill?" Loretta asked as she put her earrings away.

"I guess that's the point Romeo is trying to make. If he wouldn't harm animals, then he wouldn't harm people."

Loretta scoffed. "That's ridiculous. I know so many people out there who love their dogs or cats more than people." She stepped from the cramped bathroom to the threshold of their room. "I'm sure there are vegetarian killers out there."

Ruth couldn't argue with her friend on that. She shrugged. "Murderers are not always logical."

"Exactly." Loretta turned back toward the mirror, rummaging through items in the cabinet. "For once, we agree." Finding the tube she was looking for and a couple of round cotton pads, she tipped the bottle upside down on top of the pad and began removing the makeup from her face. Then she picked up a tube of anti-wrinkling cream, squeezing a pea-sized amount of it onto her finger, and blotted it under her eyes. As she worked on her anti-aging routine, which was long and complicated, she began to hum her favorite Streisand tune, "The Way We Were." It was a song that brought Ruth back to her younger days—much younger days. It was also a song that Loretta knew well, apparently having performed it in many of her pageants—the song was one of her talent pieces. From the stories she'd told, though, she never won a pageant, only ever placing once as runner up. Though Loretta wasn't a terrible vocalist, at least in Ruth's opinion, her singing was always a bit off and pitchy. But Loretta never cared, and it certainly never stopped her from singing and performing. She loved to sing.

Ruth finally got up, deciding that it was time for her to get ready for bed herself. She changed right in the middle of the room, grabbing her pajamas that she often left folded on her bed, and tossed her work clothes into a bag to be laundered.

The next part of Ruth's routine involved moisturizing. She went to the small desk drawer to grab her lotion, but it wasn't there. Ruth thought a moment and realized that she had gone to the beach that day, an event she hardly ever got to participate in, and she remembered that she had dropped it into her beach bag just in case.

She grabbed her bag from the closet that she had tossed it in when they got back from the beach earlier, and set it on her bed. She unsnapped the gold button that held the bag closed and paused. She put her hand to her mouth in shock, her fingertips barely touching her lips.

There, inside the bag, was the folder from the set!

"Oh no," Ruth said out loud to herself. She must've forgotten to put the folder back. Perhaps she'd gotten so wrapped up in the whirlwind of the people around her at the set that she had absent-mindedly stuck the folder in her bag. Pulling the file folder out gingerly, she looked at it, debating if she should even open it. She didn't want to invade someone's privacy. Though, she did have it open on the set as a prop while she pretended she was just another staff worker, working there, but she hadn't actually read it.

She opened it. What was the harm?

The first page was the title page. It read, "Lover's Scorn and the Secret Storm," and behind it was, "Episode 25 - Revised Ending."

Ruth furrowed her brows. Why had they revised the script? Had it been revised after Jay's death? Ruth's mind flashed back to the director and what he had said on the set that day. Something about how now that Jay was gone, he could direct the season finale how it should be done. Though, directing and rewriting a script were two entirely different things. But what if he did have it revised? Could the show's season finale be motive to kill the producer? That didn't make much sense to Ruth. What could the director possibly gain from that? Though, she'd known people to kill for much less.

She flipped to the first page and began skimming it

as Loretta was in the bathroom still humming away. As she leafed through the script, she began to realize what she really had in her hands. It wasn't just the season finale of *Darkness into Light*. This wasn't at all surprising, since that's what they were shooting on the island. It was the mere fact that she had in her hands the ending of the show, something that wouldn't be aired for another week or so, and she would be among the select few who knew the ending to the story before the rest of the world. Then she couldn't help but think of Loretta and Wanda. They would kill to get their hands on this.

Ruth continued reading. It certainly read faster than her romance novels. Even though she didn't know the backstory, it was easy for her to understand what was going on. She had to admit, it was suspenseful and exhilarating, but there was a dark, looming undertone throughout the episode. One she couldn't quite put her finger on. At only several pages from the end, she found herself holding her breath. She was at the part with the argument between Gustavo and Catalina, the one she'd overheard while on set. It was intense, and Ruth's heart was pounding.

She flipped the script faster, causing some slight wrinkles in some of the pages in her haste to find out what would happen next.

Finally, Ruth reached the end. Romeo was now barefoot on the beach at night, right outside his vacation home, staring at the stars. Someone was behind him, hiding in the shadows. Watching. Waiting.

Ruth's eyes zipped across the page.

The dark figure emerged from the shrubs of his new summer home, tiptoeing. They were sneaking up behind Romeo, but he wasn't paying attention. He didn't suspect anything. Why would he? He was too busy taking in the beach's salty air.

They were inching closer. Only several feet away. They were almost upon him now.

Ruth was eager to offer a warning. But she only read faster.

The stealthy ghost was now almost at arm's length when they stopped. A revolver raised up, glimmering in the moonlight.

Oh, no! Ruth was screaming inside her head, *Watch out!*

Bang!

Ruth gasped.

She dropped the script, and it fell onto the floor. Her mouth fell agape. It was an ending she hadn't expected. In fact, it was an ending no one would ever expect.

CHAPTER 16

"They kill Romeo?!" Loretta yelled.

"Shh." Ruth flopped her hands up and down. "Lower your voice. Someone will hear you."

Loretta ignored her, snatching the script from Ruth. "I don't believe you. They wouldn't do that." She rifled through the pages to the end and read. Eyes wide, she dropped the script. "I think I'm going to faint." She backed herself into the chair in front of the desk with the small mirror and sat down. "They can't do that!"

Ruth picked up the script. "Well, it looks like that's what they're doing."

Loretta was fanning herself with her hand. "Are you sure that's the most updated script?" It was clear Loretta was going through the stages of grief. First, denial.

Ruth flipped to the title page of the script. "It says it

right here." Ruth pointed. "'Episode Twenty-five, Revised Ending.'"

"It can't be. What will Wanda say? Oh, she will be devastated. I don't think I can tell her." Then Loretta sat up as if she'd just realized something. "Is there a date on the script? It could have been revised multiple times. How do we know that this one is the most recent update?"

Now Loretta was just grasping at straws. Ruth flipped through the pages, looking for a date, and found one stamped at the bottom of the title page. Ruth must've missed it the first time she'd looked at it.

"It's dated the day before Jay's death. It even has his initials that he personally approved it."

Loretta slouched back down into the chair, defeated again. "I don't know how I'm going to break it to Wanda."

This new bit of information meant Ruth's previous theory was out the window. No one had revised the script after Jay's death. But that only meant there was a new theory. One that she knew her friend, Loretta, would strongly oppose. But she had to go where the evidence led her.

"What if Romeo murdered Jay Juan?" Ruth asked.

Loretta let out a squeak, and she put her hand to her chest as if she were pained by the mere suggestion.

"How could you even fathom such a thing, Ruth? Romeo would never do anything of the sort."

"Just hear me out. What if Romeo was upset that he was going to be killed off the show, so he went to confront the producer, and in a fit of rage, murdered him?"

"That's ridiculous."

"Is it?"

"Where's the motive, then?"

Ruth sighed. Apparently, it was going to take a lot for Loretta to let go of her favorite actor and to see him as a possible suspect to a murder. Ruth sat down on her bed across from Loretta. "How much money does Romeo make from the show?"

"Two hundred and fifty thousand per episode."

Ruth's eyes went wide. It was much more than she thought, but it certainly helped her argument. It only took Loretta a few seconds to put it all together.

Loretta put her hands on either side of her face. "He has the perfect motive."

The next morning, Ruth was on a mission as she marched down a long corridor with the folder that held the script. The last thing anyone needed was a murderer running amok on the ship. There was no telling what they could do next, if pushed. And not to mention, justice for Jay Juan and his family, if he had one. Though, in order to capture a killer, she would need to alert the ship's security, which meant talking to the chief security officer, Harry Humphrey.

Holding the folder tighter to her chest, she walked in long strides with purpose. She would need it to prove her case, so she kept it as close to her as possible. That, and she felt an odd sense of responsibility to keep this script a secret. It was the big season finale for one of the biggest shows in the world, after all.

When she reached the end of the hall, she knocked on Humphrey's door. It took a few seconds before she heard him shout for her to come in.

Humphrey was sitting behind his desk, reading some papers that were scattered in front of him while sipping coffee from Cate's Cafe. He set the paper cup down and motioned for Ruth to come in. "What's going on, Ruth?"

His graying, light brown hair was sticking to his clammy forehead, and she couldn't help but notice the yellow pit stains on his crisp white uniform. She tried to avert her eyes from his underarms as she walked up to the desk and handed him the script.

With his head still down, he studied it. Then he looked up at Ruth over the rims of his glasses. "Is this what I think it is? Please tell me it's not what I think it is, Ruth."

"It's the script for the season finale of *Darkness into Light*."

Humphrey tossed the packet of papers on his desk between them and leaned back in his chair, crossing his arms. "C'mon, Ruth. You shouldn't have this. I don't even want to know how you obtained it."

"Well, when we stopped at Mermaid's Cay—"

"Stop, stop," Humphrey said, waving both his hands in front of him. "I don't want to know."

"It was a murder, Harry. The producer, Jay Juan, was murdered." She blurted it out, not even correcting herself when using his first name, instead of "sir."

"I know."

"You know?" Ruth gave him a confused look. "What do you mean, you know?"

"We know. We've known since the night it happened. The nasty bump on the head, the balcony door being locked."

"But you said—"

"Yeah, yeah. I know what I said to you."

"Wait." Ruth furrowed her eyebrows. "The balcony door was locked?"

"Yeah, Officer Malloy was the one who noticed it. Locked from the inside, of course. So, unless Jay was able to come back from the dead and lock the door himself, I guess we can assume someone else was there." Humphrey shook his head slowly, in disbelief. "Whoever did this wasn't too bright."

Or it was done in haste or out of rage, Ruth thought. She put her palms on his desk, leaning in. "Why didn't you tell me the truth?"

Humphrey raised his eyebrows. "That there was a murderer on the ship?" Humphrey let out a snort. Then he leaned forward, over his desk, to meet her eyes. "No way in any world was I going to tell you, Ruth."

Ruth was taken aback by Humphrey's response.

He continued, "Remember what happened the last time you knew there was a murderer on the ship?"

"Yeah, I caught them. And the one before that, too. Remember?"

"I remember you ruffling feathers with the elite, had guests in restricted areas, stalked a man on the ship, tricked another man into—"

"Okay, okay. You've made your point."

"And did you forget the chaos and the cat fight you caused between two well-respected women at the formal Mermaid's Dinner that one time?"

"All right. I get it."

"It was a complete and utter embarrassment."

"So why tell me now?"

Humphrey threw his hands up. "Because you already know. What's the point of keeping it from you if you already know, and you're going to snoop around anyway?"

Ruth remained quiet for a moment and adjusted herself. "Well, don't you want to know what happens?" she asked in a lower voice, tapping her finger on the script. "You know, the big ending?"

"No," Humphrey said, unamused. He went back to the stack of papers he'd been looking at when she came in. "But I'm sure you're going to tell me anyway."

Ruth ignored his comment. "Romeo is killed off."

Humphrey raised his eyebrows, looking at her. "And?"

Ruth let out a huff. Did she have to spell everything out for this guy? "It's motive!"

Humphrey gave her a blank stare.

Ruth was tempted to jump over the desk and start shaking the man, but instead she took a deep breath and tried again. "Do you have any idea how much he gets paid per episode?"

"Nope."

"The actor gets paid two hundred and fifty thousand dollars per episode. If he found out that Jay Juan had plans to kill him off the show, then he would be out millions." She waited for a response from

Humphrey, but it didn't come. "So, what do we do now?" she asked.

"What do we do now?" Humphrey let out a chuckle. Then he mumbled the question to himself loud enough for Ruth to hear.

She crossed her arms.

Humphrey wagged his finger between the two of them. "*We* don't do anything. *You...*" he pointed to Ruth. "You need to stay away from Romeo."

"You mean Rafael Javiera."

"Whatever his name is. In fact, stay away from all of them and just do your job. What you're paid to do. And this..." He picked the script up from his desk. "This is staying here with me."

Ruth folded her arms again.

"Now you are going to leave and go back to your kitchen," he said, voice firm.

There was no getting through to this guy. She would just have to do this on her own, just like last time. She stood and went for the door. Just as she was reaching for the knob, Humphrey spoke again, "And please, Ruth..."

Ruth turned around. Humphrey had his fingers at his temple, rubbing.

"For all things holy, stay there," he said.

"Where?"

Humphrey huffed, dropping his hands loudly on his desk in defeat. "In the kitchen!"

Ruth nodded, though she could do without his theatrics. She opened the door, but before she walked out, she said, "Oh, and by the way: Just to clarify, I didn't cause the cat fight between those two women."

Humphrey grunted, dropping his head onto his desk and waving away her words.

The man really was impossible.

CHAPTER 17

"What? You told Officer Humphrey?" Loretta began mixing a bowl of batter a little more vigorously, shaking her head. "I'm sure he was thrilled."

Ruth immediately caught onto her friend's sarcasm and added to it. "More than thrilled, he was ecstatic!"

"You're kidding?" Loretta asked.

"Unfortunately, I am."

Loretta frowned. "So, what did he say?"

"Well, first he scolded me for stealing the script. Then he rattled off all the chaos I caused the last time there was a murderer on the ship. Then he loudly prayed that I would stay in the kitchen, where I belong."

"He sounds like Ricky Ricardo."

Ruth laughed. Loretta had a way of taking her back. *I Love Lucy* was one of her favorite shows. Though, she assumed, it was everyone's favorite show. Ruth continued, "So, I was scolded, and he said that I was to stay away from everyone from *Darkness into Light*, including and most importantly the star of the show, Romeo."

"You mean, Rafael Javiera."

Ruth smiled, knowing she made the same slip-up that Humphrey had.

"But..." Loretta started.

"But, what?"

"Well, don't you think he's right? We really did create a lot of commotion the last time we were in this predicament. He may have a point."

"Have a point?! Are you seriously saying that you agree with Harry Humphrey? Humpty Dumpty Humphrey?"

Loretta burst into laughter. It was a nickname she gave Officer Humphrey the first day they met him, and it was fitting. He was short and round, and there were many times Humphrey was not only a little slow-witted but also very clumsy. "Of course not. I'm just saying he may have a point. Maybe we should be focusing on what they pay us for, which is baking and creating the best-tasting and the best-looking desserts for our guests. Not running around trying to nab a murderer," Loretta said. "I'm sorry, Ruth, but I don't recall that being anywhere in our job description."

"But we can't just let a murderer run around the ship all willy nilly."

"That's for Officer Humphrey and his team to handle. Not us."

Ruth folded her arms and tapped her foot. "Why do I have a feeling you don't want to continue investigating because your favorite star seems to be a main suspect?"

"Oh, Ruth, that's not true. I'm just saying that it isn't our job, and we could get in big trouble if we continue. Besides, you even said that Humphrey forbade you from going anywhere near Romeo."

Ruth put a finger to her chin, thinking. "So, I can't go near Romeo, and I already burned bridges with Maria Melendez. Those are the two biggest stars of the show…"

"And not to mention, Humphrey did say you can't go near *anyone* from *Darkness into Light*. I think that includes the other actors and the crew."

Loretta was right. Though, Officer Humphrey wasn't exactly her superior, either. There was a well-understood hierarchy on the ship that all crew, staff, and officers abided by. And Humphrey was a stripe—an officer.

But that didn't mean much to Ruth in the grand scheme of things. Surely, she believed in having respect for your superiors. It was something she'd taught her granddaughters, Emma and Sarah. Though, she'd also told them to respect their elders, and well, as much as Ruth hated to admit it and definitely wouldn't flaunt the fact, she was, in fact, Humphrey's elder.

Loretta stopped what she was doing and was now looking at Ruth. "Oh, no."

"What?"

"You're thinking again."

Ruth shook her head. "I'm thinking, but I'm not coming up with anything."

Loretta gasped. "Nothing? You mean to tell me Ruth Shores doesn't have a plan?"

Ruth pursed her lips. "Very funny."

"Well then, Lucy, what *are* you going to do now?"

That night, after another long day in the kitchen, Ruth and Loretta met with Wanda at the Starlight Bar. Granted, they could have gone to the crew bar, a place that was for crew and staff of the ship only. The drinks were only a dollar fifty a piece, and were mixed by amazing bartenders aboard the ship, but Ruth paid the extra money to be outside on deck fifteen, under the stars and surrounded by the ocean night air. She'd rather be away from work as much as possible, since the crew bar was on the third level of the ship and was mostly for the younger staff workers anyway. The parties there were known to get extremely crazy, and Ruth would rather not get involved in some of the affairs and trouble that took place in there. Guests of the ship were also forbidden from the crew bar, but rumor had it that even officers had snuck passengers down there, an offense Ruth didn't particularly want to be involved with or witness, just in case security investigated it. That would cause a whole new scenario of problems and quite a dilemma. She wasn't particularly fond of the idea of snitching on her fellow co-workers, or worse, an officer of the ship. But she wasn't one for lying either—if she could help it, that is.

Ruth turned her attention to Wanda, who was checking her watch. It was the fifth time she'd done that, not that Ruth was counting. Wanda was dressed in a glittery, royal-blue blazer with dangling gold earrings and more makeup than Maria Melendez herself. Ruth had a nagging suspicion that it had something to do with the handsome new guy Wanda had followed to Bingo.

"You told Officer Humphrey?" Wanda said, scrunching up her face. "What were you thinking?"

"I was thinking he would do his job and look further into it."

"Oh, well, that wouldn't be as much fun then. Humphrey is by the book and all about covering up anything that may give the cruise ship a bad rap. It's his job." Wanda gave a shrug, then added, "So, where's the script? I'd like to read it."

"No," both Ruth and Loretta said in unison. They couldn't tell Wanda that Romeo was killed off. She would lose her mind. Then Loretta added, "You don't want to read it anyway. Then it wouldn't be a surprise."

"Besides," Ruth said. "Officer Humphrey confiscated it."

Wanda slapped the palm of her hand onto the bar. "What? You let Hungry, Hungry Humphrey take it?"

"I had no choice."

"A shame and, if I may add, devastating news." Wanda paused. "Well, then, how did it end?"

"Like I said," Loretta chimed in, "it wouldn't be a surprise."

Ruth cut in quickly, trying to redirect Wanda's attention to something else. "So, let's go over the list of suspects."

Wanda set down her drink. "Let's see, we have the

director guy, Frederick Scott, who was fighting with Jay Juan the night of his death. Maria Melendez, whom you, Ruth, overheard talking to someone, threatening his life, presumably. And..." Wanda paused, thinking.

Loretta continued, "There's the co-executive producer, Hector, who was next in line for Jay's job, and was living in his shadows as he wrote the episodes while Jay took full credit for them."

Ruth noticed Wanda was checking her watch again. Was this the sixth time now?

Loretta continued, "And of course, now we have Ra—"

"Radically come up with new theories," Ruth interrupted her friend. She couldn't let slip that it was Rafael —Romeo—to Wanda. She would do more than just pitch a fit.

Wanda looked up. "Huh?"

"You know, try to tie some of these suspects to a theory." Ruth nervously downed a few gulps of her martini and swallowed hard.

Wanda nodded as if she understood Ruth. Then she checked her watch again.

"Waiting for someone?" Ruth asked.

Wanda covered the face of her watch with her hand. "No." She picked up her martini glass and took a sip. "What makes you think that?"

"The darker shade of lipstick, the lining done around your eyes, the outfit, the extra hairspray—which I didn't think was possible."

Loretta tried to touch Wanda's hair, but Wanda pulled back just in time. She palmed her own hair, making sure it wasn't disturbed. Loretta chuckled. "It's like a shield. You could catch a bullet in that."

"And, not to mention, you've been checking the time more than my granddaughters check their cellphones," Ruth pointed out.

A tall, handsome man with broad shoulders walked up toward them. "Ah, Wanda De la Rue," he said in a deep baritone voice.

Ruth and Loretta mouthed "De la Rue" with scrunched up and perplexed faces. Wanda's last name was Buckets. An unfortunate name, surely, but it was her surname, nonetheless. Wanda gave them a look to keep quiet.

The distinguished-looking man took Wanda's hand. "You look enchanting."

Loretta stifled a soft chuckle, then cleared her throat.

The man turned to them and said, "And who are your lovely friends?"

"Them? Oh, how rude of me."

Ruth raised an eyebrow. This was clearly not the blunt, bossy Wanda she knew.

Wanda motioned toward Ruth and Loretta. "These are my friends, Ruth Shores and Loretta Moran." Wanda then regarded her friends. "This is Norman Badeaux."

"Ah, a French man," Loretta said.

Norman smiled. "You can just call me Norm."

"Hi," Ruth said, shaking his hand.

"Pleasure to make your acquaintance," Loretta said, holding out her hand.

The man beamed, showing his perfectly aligned teeth. "Wanda, dear, I was going to ask you to join me for dinner. Are you hungry?"

Wanda giggled girlishly and nodded.

Norm shifted his gaze toward Ruth and Loretta. "Maybe your friends would like to join us? I'm buying." He gave them a wink.

"Oh, no. I'm sure they'd rather—" Wanda started.

Loretta cut in, "We'd love to!" Wanda nudged Loretta with her elbow, an obvious attempt to tell her to shut up that even Ruth noticed. But if Ruth knew one thing about her friend Loretta, it was that she never turned down a free dinner. Ever.

"Great. I was thinking the Blue Dolphin," Norm said. "I hear they have great steaks."

Loretta had already grabbed her scarf and purse before they could come to a consensus, and she pointed to the door leading to the elevators. "Let's go!"

Wanda rolled her eyes in disapproval, but there was nothing anyone could say. Loretta had apparently made the final decision for everyone. They were going to join Norm and Wanda for dinner at the classy Blue Dolphin restaurant.

CHAPTER 18

The Blue Dolphin was an upscale restaurant with dark blue tablecloths and runners the color of icecaps. A small tea candle accentuated each table, adding a simple yet elegant touch. A waiter, young enough to be any of their grandsons, came bearing four imitation leather-bound menus. He had dark hair, mouse-like features, and a name tag that read, "Jonah." Ruth thought it was a lovely name.

"Would you like to make your drink order?" he asked.

Norm opened his menu and pulled it back, apparently farsighted. He pointed to something within. Jonah leaned forward to get a better look. "We'll have a bottle of wine," Norm said. He looked up at the three women, regarding them next, "If that's okay with all of you, of course."

They all nodded. Who were they to argue with a man who was paying for everything and wanted to order a bottle of wine?

"A red should do the trick. The Cabernet Sauvignon."

Ruth would have chosen the Merlot herself, but Cabernet Sauvignon was a close second. Though, he could have picked any red wine and Ruth would have been happy.

Norm offered the ladies to order first. There weren't many entrées listed, but that was expected in an upscale restaurant such as the Blue Dolphin. There were five main dishes and a couple of salad and pasta choices.

Loretta, sitting on the other side of Norm, opposite of Wanda, spoke first. She ordered the filet mignon stuffed with crab meat and topped with a creamy white herb sauce. Ruth, next to Loretta and across from Norm, ordered stuffed shrimp with rice pilaf and sweet vermouth shrimp butter.

Everyone looked at Wanda, waiting for her order. She scanned the menu and then shifted her gaze over the top of it. "I'm still deciding. Norm, why don't you go ahead and order."

"Hm, well, I've heard an awful lot about the Beef Wellington here."

"Yes, sir," the waiter said. "Chef Rimsley is especially known for the Beef Wellington dish."

Chef Jordan Rimsley, a famous chef and TV personality, seemed to have made a career of berating other cooks for entertainment. Of course, Chef Rimsley wouldn't be personally preparing the dishes—this restaurant was simply among the chains he owned and promoted often on his shows.

"Well, you don't have to twist my arm anymore," Norm said. "I'll have that."

"Very well, sir."

"Me too," Wanda said, closing her menu. "That sounds delightful."

"Good choice, ma'am," Jonah said before taking their menus. He scurried away with their orders, sashaying between the tables to the kitchen and bursting through the double swinging doors before he disappeared.

Norm regarded the ladies. "So, you all work on the ship?"

They all nodded.

"What's it like constantly traveling?"

"Well," Ruth started, "it's not like a vacation. We work every day."

"No days off?"

"Nope."

The waiter came back with the wine and side salads, interrupting the conversation for several moments.

Norm put his elbows on the table, and Ruth couldn't help but think of her free-spirited granddaughter, Emma. She had a habit of putting her elbows on the table, a habit Ruth struggled to break her from.

"That's got to be hard," Norm said.

"What must be hard?" Ruth asked.

"Not ever getting a day off."

"Oh." Ruth flapped her hand. "You get used to it."

"And it's easier to take naps," Loretta added, unfolding the cloth napkin and laying it on her lap. "You learn to fall asleep in a matter of seconds after a few weeks. It's actually quite astonishing how that happens."

Norm picked up his fork, stabbing a piece of tomato. "I could only imagine." He popped the tomato in his mouth.

Everyone was quiet for a moment, and Ruth could sense the awkwardness. It was something she hated. She didn't like feeling uncomfortable, and she looked at Wanda, who was sliding the fork from her mouth and eyeing up Norm.

Ruth looked at Norm. "So, are you here with family?"

"No." Norm dabbed his mouth with his napkin. "No, no. I'm a widower of seven years."

"Oh, I'm so sorry to hear," Ruth said.

"I'm not," Wanda remarked quietly for only Ruth to hear. Ruth kicked her under the table.

"Don't be," he said. "I'm quite all right now. Mary was a great wife, but she hated to travel. She would get homesick the moment we left town. This trip was long awaited. And now, I'm an eligible bachelor, taking in the fresh ocean air, the night stars, and"—he lifted his glass—"the alcohol. Who could ask for more? Don't get me wrong. I loved my wife, still do, and I miss her. But there's no point in dwelling in the past. We must keep living."

"Hear, hear," Wanda said, lifting her glass.

Ruth rolled her eyes. Wanda was impossible at times. She was a woman who lived for the moment, and didn't allow anyone to push her around, even her own friends. It was something to admire, but at times, it also reminded Ruth how insensitive Wanda could be.

Norm smiled. He clinked his glass to hers and waited for Ruth and Loretta to join, clinking his glass next to theirs too. Ruth had a passing and disturbing thought. Was this man looking for a harem? She looked around the room to see if anyone recognized that the man was sitting at a table with three women, but no one seemed to notice. Regardless, after ordering another bottle of wine and having a few more full glasses of alcohol, Ruth was really enjoying the man's company and so were the other women, including Wanda, even though they had crashed her romantic dinner with him. There were jokes and laughter as they all shared stories about their families, including grandchildren.

"My grandson keeps signing me up to these new social platform things online." Norm laughed, taking another sip of his wine. "I try to be a hip grandpa and keep up with the times, but this online stuff is just too much. What's with all the beeps and jingles? I mean, I shut it down and it still whistles at me."

"Me too." Ruth pointed at him while holding her half-empty glass. "I was just telling Loretta how my granddaughter signed me up to that Friendbook thing, and I couldn't get the beeping to stop."

They all laughed, obviously tipsy.

"They're called alerts," Loretta said.

"Well," Norm said, setting down his glass. "He needs to stop adding me to the Friendbook groups. Ugh, they are the most frustrating."

"Group?" Ruth gasped.

Norm gave Ruth a confused look. "Yeah, that's what I said. Group or groups or whatever they're called." He laughed again.

"Loretta, that's it!" Ruth said.

"What?" Though Ruth was referring to Loretta, both Loretta and Wanda gave her a perplexed look.

"What is it, ole yeller?" Loretta said, jokingly.

Ruth would have batted her friend's shoulder playfully but she was too busy, mind reeling. "The group!"

Everyone looked at Ruth, confused.

"Loretta, the *Darkness into Light* group. The one that Romeo does behind the scenes. That's how I can investigate the murder. Maybe Rafael recorded a behind-the-scenes video the night of the murder."

Norm's smile faded quickly. "Murder? What murder?" he asked, seriously concerned. It was obvious he knew nothing about a murder. The only ones who seemed to know about it were the people closest to *Darkness into Light* and everyone off the ship, since it had probably hit the newspapers, media, and internet faster than a torch browning a meringue topping.

Wanda waved off her friends. "Nothing. Don't listen to them."

"So, there *was* a murder." His face was whiter than a pre-torched meringue.

※

"What is wrong with you two?" Wanda asked. "You always have to chase off my boyfriends."

Wanda was fuming. When Norm found out about the murder, he'd immediately paid the bill and left.

Wanda had called after him, but he left them all—with a five-star dinner. But neither Ruth nor Loretta—nor Wanda, for that matter—were complaining. They all stayed to enjoy the rest of their dinner.

"Can't help it that the guy is so sensitive," Loretta said, shoveling another juicy bite of her filet mignon into her mouth. They all had to admit, Chef Rimsley's staff was amazing. "Besides, what are you complaining about? We got a free dinner out of it."

Wanda shook her head, but not without taking another bite of her food too.

"We don't always chase off your boyfriends," Ruth added, taking a sip of her wine.

"I just thought Norm could be the one," Wanda said.

"All that aside, we need to focus," Ruth started. "We have to watch the behind-the-scenes with Romeo—er, Rafael. See if we can find any clues."

"I've watched them all," Loretta said. "There's nothing in them, I promise you."

"Well, I want to see them. Maybe you missed something."

"Seems to me you're searching under rocks," Loretta said.

"Loretta," Wanda said, "if she wants to watch Romeo's behind-the-scenes videos, why don't you let her? I wouldn't mind watching them myself," she added, waggling her eyebrows. "I mean, what's the harm?"

"What's the harm?" Loretta asked. "You want to tell her, or should I?"

Ruth shook her head. "Don't, Loretta—"

"Our friend, the sleuth here, thinks the murderer could be Rafael Javiera."

Wanda clutched her chest. "Romeo?! Are you insane?!"

"No," Ruth said, knowing the jig was up. She looked at Loretta. "Fine, you want to tell her everything, then why don't you just go right ahead!"

Loretta shook her head vigorously. It was just like her to start drama and then not be bold enough to finish it by revealing the most shocking details.

"Tell me what?" Wanda asked, swiveling her head between the two women.

"The big ending of *Darkness into Light*," Ruth said, trying to avoid eye contact with Wanda.

"Well, out with it!" Wanda's eyes were wide with anticipation.

Ruth spoke first. "Romeo is killed."

"What?!" Wanda screamed. Some of the patrons shot them irritated stares.

"Keep your voice down," Loretta said, looking around the restaurant. "No one's supposed to know."

Wanda repeated herself, only this time in a harsh whisper, then asked, "Was this the plan all along?"

"It was a rewrite done the day before Jay's death," Loretta said.

Wanda put her face in her hands. "Tell me it's not true."

"That's why we are thinking Romeo could be a prime suspect to Jay's death," Ruth said.

Wanda popped her head up out of her hands. "Are you insane?!"

"We have to go where the evidence leads us," Ruth said gently.

Wanda got up, throwing her napkin down on the table. "I don't have to listen to this nonsense."

Ruth glanced up at the woman. "Wanda, please sit down."

"No," she said, crossing her arms. "What in the world makes you think he would've done something like this? What evidence do you even have?"

"Well, for one, he gets paid a quarter million dollars per episode."

Wanda plopped back down in her seat. "That's a pretty good motive," she said, defeated.

"That's what we are saying. His act could be just that. He's a great actor, very talented. What if his life on camera and on this ship is all just an act?"

"I can't believe this," Wanda said, still in shock. "Not my sweet, gorgeous Romeo. Don't take him away from me too!"

"Don't be so dramatic," Loretta said, downing the last of her wine.

Ruth looked at her friend, crinkling her forehead. "Speak for yourself."

Loretta shot her a stony glare.

"So, now what do we do?" Wanda asked.

Ruth finished her own wine and set the glass on the table. "We check the behind-the-scenes videos for any clues."

CHAPTER 19

In the Orca Internet Cafe, Ruth and Wanda were huddled around one of the computers while Loretta entered her username and password to her internet account. It was the next day, and Ruth and Loretta were exhausted. They had gotten up several hours early to do prep work in the kitchen before meeting Wanda at the Cafe. Wanda didn't have to be at work until later in the afternoon, since they were at port at the last island and most of the passengers would be enjoying their sunny day on the beach or shopping. So, Wanda had appointed her co-worker, Eileen, to watch over the empty salon. Ruth knew the southern bird wouldn't mind. She could only imagine her powder-pink lips pouting as her tongue wrestled a wad of gum while she spent the entire day flipping through a steamy romance novel.

Loretta logged into her Friendbook account. Once she was in, she paused. "The internet costs about a dollar a minute. Who's going to pay me for this?"

"It doesn't cost that much," Wanda said.

Loretta sank into her chair slightly, crossing her arms. "Yes, it does." She was right, though it wasn't quite a dollar a minute. It was a little more than half that, even for the crew members. And, the cruise line banked on the spotty, slow internet as well, since satellite connections were spread pretty thin on the water. It was a great way for them to make even more money while users waited for pages to load and freeze up.

"Loretta, calm down," Ruth said. "We'll all chip in."

"Sure," Wanda added, though Ruth wasn't confident they could count on her share—she still owed Ruth fifty bucks she'd borrowed.

Loretta sat up straight, clicking and scrolling. Ruth caught glimpses of photos of smiling faces before Loretta clicked on a group page. Romeo's profile picture sprouted on the left corner of the screen. As Loretta scrolled some more, she said, "Okay, so here are the behind-the-scenes videos. Which one should we look at first?"

Ruth hadn't thought about that. She wasn't sure how

all of this worked, never really what they would call "tech savvy"—a term her granddaughters had used. "Where's the latest one?" Ruth asked. "Maybe we should look at that one first."

"His latest one was..." Loretta stopped.

"What?"

"That's odd," Loretta said. "The last one was the night of Jay's murder, and it was just uploaded five hours ago."

Ruth and Wanda leaned in closer, waiting.

"Well," Wanda said anxiously. "Play it."

Loretta clicked on the thumbnail. The video was shaky, and Ruth could tell immediately that whoever was holding the camera was in the hallway on deck seventeen. The decor, different carpeting, and the distance between each door was a dead giveaway, not to mention the swarms of sea officers. Then the camera swiveled to show Romeo's face—mostly his chin and up his nose, not the most flattering angle. "My friends," he said in a low voice, almost a whisper. "I just got word that Jay Juan, the producer of *Darkness into Light*, fell overboard while on our way to our set on one of the Bahama islands." Then he looked down the hall and covered his mouth with his hand.

Loretta paused the video and raised her eyebrows. "I don't know, but he seems rather upset."

"He could be one of those murderers who returns to

the scene of the crime," Ruth said. "Sometimes, they even offer to help. We can't count him out yet."

Wanda looked perplexed, tilting her head slightly to one side.

"What do you think, Wanda?" Ruth asked.

She was still staring at Romeo's frozen image on the screen. "I'm just wondering how he can use the most unflattering angle and still look good."

"Oh," Ruth said, batting her friend on the shoulder lightly. "Let's just continue the video."

Loretta clicked on it again, and it began to play. Romeo turned the camera so that the viewers could see the hallway and all the officers walking in and out of the cabin. As he inched closer to the room, Ruth could see that they had the door propped open so the officers could have easier access. As Romeo approached the open cabin, the women leaned in even closer. He turned the corner into the foyer. Straight ahead was a painting of a woman in pink and the same iceberg blue as the runners and matching artwork in the Blue Dolphin restaurant.

Romeo stepped to the right, giving them a full and clear shot of Jay Juan's cabin. It was breathtaking, and Ruth couldn't imagine one man staying in the suite—it was made for at least a family, maybe two. Though, it wasn't the first time Ruth had ever seen the suite. She'd seen it during a tour before she began working on the ship, but she'd also been there right after she'd seen Jay go overboard. She just hadn't had a chance to really take it all in with all the chaos.

On the right, there was a leather couch that Ruth could only assume could be turned into a double sofa bed. There were hardwood floors with modern rugs in the living area and the study, and a big-screen TV mounted on the wall, complete with modern decor and metal end tables with glass tops. Off to the left, in the study, sat a white marble desk that matched the dining room table. The desk seemed to be used the most in the suite, as it had small heaps of folders and papers and a laptop.

"The man seemed hard at work, even on a cruise," Ruth said.

Loretta turned to Ruth. "He was at work. It wasn't supposed to be a vacation."

"You're right. I'm just not used to seeing the desks in the cabins being used to hold piles of paperwork, I guess."

The women returned their attention to the computer screen. Behind the study was where all the action was. The door to the balcony was directly behind the desk, and it was wide open, where officers and stripes could be seen flooding the area, walking in and out of the balcony's glass doors.

Before anyone could say a word, Officer Humphrey appeared in the video, coming back into the suite. Almost immediately, he noticed Romeo, though it felt like he had noticed the three women too, hiding behind the computer screen as they watched the scene unfold.

"Darn!" Loretta said. "We're caught."

They were all still staring at the screen when Humphrey approached Romeo with his hands up in front of his chest, waving. "No one is allowed in here."

"But I'm Rafael Javiera. I play Romeo in *Darkness into Light*. This is my producer's suite. What is going on?"

"Sir, are you recording with your phone?" Humphrey asked.

Now the women were staring at the fine wood grain of the floor and the intricate fibers of Romeo's pant leg as he adjusted his phone. "No," they could hear Romeo say.

"Are you sure?"

"Yes, I was about to take a picture before you caught me."

There was a moment of silence, and the women were still watching the wood floor.

"Sir, I'm going to have to ask you to leave," Humphrey said. "This area is off limits."

"But my producer...I heard he went overboard."

"As soon as we know something, we will let you know. Now, allow me to escort you out." The camera was moving, heading for the foyer. Humphrey's voice came over the speakers again, "Try to get some rest. And if we find any new information, we will let you know. Good night, sir."

A few moments later, Romeo looked into the camera. He was now walking back down the hall he had come from. "Phew," he said. "That was close." And the video froze, and then all went black.

"What happened?" Wanda asked.

Loretta glanced at Wanda. "Nothing. It's the end of the video."

"That's it?"

"I guess so," Ruth said.

Wanda huffed. "Well, that wasn't telling at all."

"It wasn't meant to be," Loretta said.

Ruth broke in. "Let's watch another."

"Should we watch the one right before this one?" Loretta asked.

"I think that's a great idea."

"It will also make it easier since this shows the latest videos on the top. We'll just work our way down."

The second video was of all the cast, including Jay and Hector, in Jay's suite the first day of the cruise trip.

It was similar to the party they had after winning the Telly Award, only this time, they weren't in suits and glittery gowns. Instead, they were dressed more business casual. There was champagne in tall glasses, and many of them were hooting and laughing. Maria could be seen in the corner, wearing a white pantsuit, talking on her cellphone. She seemed wound up, like the person on the other line was ruffling her feathers. Then Romeo zoomed his camera for a close-up shot of the Telly Award on Jay's desk. "He brings that thing with him everywhere he goes," Romeo said.

Then Jay cut in, "It's my pride sitting there. I don't go anywhere without it, and I always like to place it somewhere where I can see it, like my desk. Gives me the motivation I need to work even harder on the scripts so that, one day soon, the Telly can have a companion."

Hector, the co-executive producer, could be seen downing the rest of his drink and then he poured himself another tall glass of champagne. Ruth couldn't help but suspect Hector more after seeing this. She could only recall the rumor that he had been the one who was writing the scripts, and it was Jay who was taking the credit. She logged what she had just seen into the back of her mind for safe keeping.

They watched several more videos. One showed them back at their original set, which would have been a couple of days before the cruise. Romeo was giving his viewers a tour of the back area behind the set, including the dressing rooms. After showing everyone Jay Juan's office door, the blonde woman who played Catalina burst out with a folder in her hand.

"What's wrong?" Romeo asked as he approached her.

Her face relaxed at the sight of Romeo. She shook her head. "Nothing." Then the video went to black.

"Huh, wonder what was wrong?" Ruth said.

Wanda shrugged. "I don't know. But I'm sure Romeo took care of it. He's such a gentleman."

Both women looked at Wanda.

Wanda's eyes jumped back and forth between both of her friends. "What? We haven't proven he's a murderer or anything," Wanda added, tilting her chin up at them. "I'm allowed to think he's a gentleman."

They watched a few more videos, but there was nothing more they could find that was even the least bit suspicious or clued them in to anything.

Loretta sighed, looking at the time. "We'd better wrap this up. It's nearly been an hour. This is going to cost an arm and a leg."

Wanda yawned. "She's right. I best get back to the salon anyway. Start getting ready for the passengers to head on back in and ask me to wash out the sand and grit from their hair and from under their nails." She got up, grabbing her bag and hauling the massive thing over her shoulder.

Ruth watched her friend leave. She couldn't help but run over the questions that were nagging her in the back of her mind. Why was Romeo trying to snoop around Jay's suite the night of his murder? Was he returning to the scene of the crime? A crime he committed after learning he'd been written off the show? Or was it Maria? She seemed to keep a great distance from Jay, especially when he was in the same room, while everyone else seemed to enjoy his parties. Except Hector, that is. The man seemed awfully uncomfortable and upset, especially after Jay's comment about working hard and writing the scripts for the show, when they all knew it was Hector who was writing the show's episodes. And what about Catalina? What was she so upset about after leaving Jay's office? What had happened in there? Ruth seemed to have more questions than answers after watching the behind-the-scenes footage.

"You ready to go back to the kitchen?" Loretta asked, interrupting Ruth's thoughts.

Ruth nodded.

As they made their way to the kitchen, one thing was certain: these questions were going to bother her the rest of the day.

CHAPTER 20

Back in the kitchen, Ruth and Loretta were working on a batch of triple-chocolate cupcakes with John, and Ruth couldn't keep her mind from reeling. She picked up another naked cupcake and piped chocolate frosting on top of it in a swirl, then set it down on the other side of her. John added a drizzle of chocolate sauce and topped it with sprinkles, while Loretta added a square piece of smooth dark chocolate on top. Ruth picked up another cupcake. "We need to talk to Hector."

"Hector?" Loretta asked, placing another square piece of chocolate atop another cupcake. "Why?"

"Didn't you see how he responded to Jay's comment about working hard on the scripts?"

Loretta shook her head.

Ruth continued, "He drank his entire glass of champagne and then poured himself more."

"So? I'd do the same if I were offered free champagne."

"Don't you see, Loretta? He has one of the biggest motives. He's right up there with Romeo."

"How so?"

"He writes the scripts, and Jay takes all the credit. You know how that would make you feel, especially if it's one of the top shows."

"And don't forget that he was also next in line to get Jay's job," John added.

Ruth looked at Loretta with pleading eyes.

Loretta put a finger to her chin. "I guess I hadn't thought about all that. I suppose this would be better than Romeo being in the hot seat as the most likely suspect."

"Don't get too excited," Ruth said. "He's definitely not off the hook. He has just as big if not a bigger motive to kill Jay. I just can't go near the actor."

"You can't go near any of them, remember?"

"You mean, I can't get caught being near any of them, and I think that rule only applies on the ship. On an island, it's a different story."

"Or like the crew bar," John said. "What happens at the crew bar stays at the crew bar. It's like another zip code. Which could definitely be applied to an island." John smiled, then added, "What happens on the island, stays on the island."

Ruth grinned. "Exactly."

※

Ruth was clomping through the atrium with her sunhat and glasses. She had decided to change as if she were going to the beach just like the last time. She had on her one-piece, nautical bathing suit and a wispy white coverup, complete with a bag. But not the beach bag she'd brought last time. No way. She wasn't going to roam around an island hauling a big bag. This time, she brought her hobo straw tote bag, with a black-and-white polka dot scarf tied around the handle, to hold only her essentials.

As she got closer to the exit, Gerald was about to greet her as if she were a guest on the ship, when he recognized her. "Ruthie, another outing? That's two in one trip. How are you able to pull that off?"

Ruth's painted lips stretched to either side. "Gerald, you should know by now I can manage anything if I really want to."

"Please tell me you're not on your way to trouble again?"

Ruth swatted him on the shoulder. "How could you think such a thing?"

Gerald smiled, showing off his dimples. He was a very handsome man. She just wished he would ease up on the hair gel. She could smell it a mile away, and it was overwhelming. "Sorry, ma'am." He gave a slight bow. "You have a beautiful day."

"Thank you, sir." She gave him another smile, enjoying their little banter.

She made her way out onto the gangway and set her sights on finding Hector. She searched through the shops for about a half hour before it dawned on her that he probably wasn't here to shop, and he probably got all of his clothes personally tailored for him anyway. She decided to go to the beach. Maybe she'd find him there, swimming or boarding. When she finally reached the sand, she took off her shoes and ambled toward the water, where all the sunbathers and readers were, enjoying the midday sun. She walked along the beach with no luck. She knew it would be hard to find him on the island, but for some reason, she felt like if she tried hard enough, she would definitely find him. After another hour of searching, she was exhausted. She was weaving around people lying on towels under umbrellas when she finally stumbled across someone familiar. It was Hector. He was wearing a woven straw hat to block the sun from his eyes and reading what looked like a script, marking it up with a red pen.

"Hi there," Ruth said.

The man looked up over his sunglasses. "Hi. Can I help you?"

"You're Hector, right?"

The man just stared at her for a moment.

"You write for *Darkness into Light*. I mean, that's what I've heard."

The man couldn't help but crack a smile. "Yes. I've been writing the episodes for *Darkness into Light* since Episode One."

"I thought so. Many people think that Jay does the writing for the show, but I read that you are actually the genius behind it." Ruth craned her neck to look at what script he was holding. "Are you working on something there?"

"Oh, yeah, I'm just reworking a new script for the next season. I like to edit my own work several times before submission."

"I heard you're taking over the show. You know, taking over Jay's job."

"You know about that already?"

"Yeah, I work on the ship. I'm not really supposed to be talking to you, I guess." Ruth giggled. "But I had to meet *the* Hector, er..." Ruth couldn't remember his last name. She had to think fast. "Uh, writer behind the show." Ruth took a breath of relief for her quick save. If there was one thing Ruth was good at, it was improvising and knowing what to say to butter a person up enough to confide in her.

"I just so happened to be working the night it happened," Ruth continued. "So, to answer your question—yes, I know. It was unfortunate. Though, I heard now that they are considering foul play."

"I heard the same. They've been giving me updates on everything."

"Oh, they have?" *Of course, they are,* Ruth thought. Leave it to Officer Humphrey and his team to botch a murder investigation by giving away everything to a likely suspect.

"Of course, they have. I'm the co-executive producer. Or, now, the executive producer."

"Yes, you were next in line to run the show."

Hector paused, staring at her intently. Then he closed the script he was working on and pulled his glasses up to really look at Ruth. "Ah, there it is."

Ruth gave him a confused look. "What?"

"That look." He pointed at her with his pen. "As if I did it."

Ruth shook her head.

"Ever since Jay passed, even my own co-workers

have been giving me that same accusing look."

"Who?" Ruth asked.

"Sure," Hector said, ignoring her question. "I was next in line for Jay's job, and he took credit for my writing, but that was part of the deal."

"Deal?"

"Yes, deal. The one we agreed upon when I signed on with him to do the show. He loved the idea, but because I didn't know what I was doing, he made himself the producer and me the co-producer. It only made sense to have a person who knew the business to be the frontrunner of the show. Sure, after a while, it bothered me once I really started learning the ropes of the job, but I didn't kill him. If it wasn't for him, I wouldn't be where I am today. I'd still be in my dingy little apartment, still writing, barely able to make ends meet. He gave me the opportunity of my life. So, I'm going to tell you the same as I told them: It wasn't me, and I have proof."

"Proof?" Ruth asked. Then she let out a nervous chuckle. "I don't need proof. It's okay." The words came out before she could stop them. It was her politeness taking over. She didn't actually mean it. She wanted the proof. She was interested in his proof.

Hector pulled his wallet out of his pocket, opening it up. He filed through it before he pulled out a small slip of paper and held it up for Ruth to see. It took her a moment to realize what it was. It was a theater ticket for one of the musicals they held on the ship.

"See." He pointed to the date and time. "After the meet-and-greet, I went to this show with my girlfriend, and I didn't get out until almost twenty minutes after they'd found Jay's body."

Ruth took a closer look at the ticket, realizing he was right. He put the stub back in his wallet for keepsake.

"She wasn't allowed to stay with me in my cabin because Jay didn't want family or friends on the cruise with us. It was supposed to be work only. But I wanted her to come on the cruise, and so I paid for her stateroom. I met her at the theater after the meet-and-greet. Luckily, I forgot to throw away my ticket stub, and so I was exonerated almost immediately when the officers questioned me. I have witnesses who saw me there and everything."

"I didn't mean to—" Ruth started, but Hector continued, cutting her off.

"Was I mildly agitated that Jay continued to get all the credit for the creation of the show? Yes. Did I hate the guy? Sometimes. Did I kill the man? No. Now, if you don't mind"—he tapped the new script with his red pen—"I have work to do." He flipped open the script, leaned back in his chair, and began reading it, ignoring Ruth's presence.

CHAPTER 21

Ruth felt embarrassed. Beyond embarrassed. She walked back to her cabin in defeat and utter humiliation. When she entered the cabin, Loretta was fixing herself up in the bathroom again. She was singing until she heard Ruth enter. When she came out, she appeared taken aback by Ruth's mood. "I assume it didn't go well. You look like a wounded cat crawling back to your hole."

"Thanks," Ruth said, tossing her bag onto her bed. "I made a total fool of myself."

Loretta chuckled playfully. "Well, that's nothing new. You always had a knack for that."

Ruth glared at her. Loretta's smile disappeared instantly, and her face softened. "You want to talk about it?" Loretta asked.

"No, the wound to my pride is still too fresh." She lay back onto her bed.

"So, it's safe to assume that Hector isn't the murderer?"

"Nope. He has a solid alibi, complete with witnesses." Ruth sighed. "What are we missing?" Ruth thought a moment, then sprang back up to face Loretta. "Maybe we should take another look at the videos."

"Romeo's behind-the-scenes videos?"

Ruth nodded. "There must be so many hidden things in those videos. And with new information, maybe I can make a little more sense out of the clips."

Loretta shook her head. "I'm heading out tonight. Going to enjoy my hours off, relaxing, drinking, and possibly gambling. Maybe I'll meet a nice bachelor myself, like Wanda did. Wake up the next morning with regrets." Loretta turned to walk back to the bathroom. "You should go enjoy yourself too."

"C'mon, Loretta. We're so close to figuring this thing out."

"No way," Loretta said as she rummaged through the clothes hanging in the closet.

Ruth flopped back onto her bed.

"You need a hobby," Loretta said. After a moment, she sighed, dropping her hands at her sides. She walked back over to Ruth. "Okay, here's what we'll do. I'll log you into my account…"

Ruth propped herself up with her elbows. "Really?"

"Only with the agreement that you pay for the services you use. In full." Loretta stressed the last two words. "And you can bore yourself all you want with videos we've already seen, and I can go party." Loretta did a little jig to give a glimpse of what it looked like when she partied.

Ruth laughed. "Sounds fair to me."

"All right," Loretta said. "Let's go."

They walked to the Orca Internet Cafe. It was empty, but the computers were still on. Loretta took the same computer they had used last time when Wanda was with them and began logging in. She pulled up Romeo's Friendbook group for Ruth, which Ruth was grateful for, since she wasn't sure she knew how to navigate the social media site. She barely knew how to check her email. "There you are," Loretta said, pushing herself from the table and giving up her seat to Ruth. "I have all the videos up, and the most recent ones are on top. Dates are under each video as well, if you need it."

Ruth plopped down and thanked her friend.

"And this is a mouse…" Loretta started.

Ruth swatted her away. "I know what a mouse is."

Loretta laughed as she walked toward the door. "Have fun. I know *I* will."

Ruth smiled at her friend. Once Loretta was gone, she began scrolling down the page. She re-watched a couple of videos before deciding that she should narrow her search, focusing on clips with Jay in them. There wasn't anything she could find in those clips that she hadn't already found, so she tried to find anything with Maria on-screen, but found almost nothing. The woman was always busy in the background on her cellphone, either texting, talking, or taking a selfie. *Not very helpful*, Ruth thought. Then she came up with a new plan to just watch the videos in order, starting a week before the cast boarded the ship. This meant she'd have to watch a little over twenty videos, including the ones Romeo had recorded and uploaded after they left port. Ruth crinkled her brows. Did this guy have a life outside *Darkness into Light* or Friendbook? She sighed and began the excruciating task.

Halfway through the videos, Ruth felt her eyes grow heavy. She shook the sleepiness away and narrowed her eyes toward the screen. "There's got to be something in one of these videos," she said to herself. "Something I'm missing." After several more videos, her head dipped, startling her enough to wake up again.

Just then, she heard Loretta's voice. "Ruth, you need to get some sleep."

"Huh?" she said, turning toward the voice. "What time is it?"

"Late. Very late. I went back to the cabin, expecting you to be there sleeping, but here you are, still watching videos."

Ruth looked at her watch. "My! Where did the time go? I now see how my granddaughters can stare at a computer screen for hours."

"I'm worried about you. You haven't gotten much sleep the last few nights. Maybe it's time to let this go before your health starts to decline."

Ruth nodded. It wasn't that she agreed with her friend completely. She was just too tired to argue.

"Did you even find anything?" Loretta asked.

"Not really. I tried to focus on videos that had Jay in them, but there wasn't much, so I expanded my search, going through all the videos again."

"Better you than me. All Jay seems to talk about is his Telly Award. I mean, we get it…"

Ruth perked up, putting up a finger.

"What?" Loretta asked, confused.

"The Telly Award." Ruth turned back to the computer.

Loretta cocked her head, watching Ruth. She scrolled

up to the most recent video, Romeo in Jay's suite the night of his murder, and clicked on it. It showed Romeo's face in that awkward angle again, an image that was now almost imprinted in Ruth's memory. The camera went down the hallway into Jay's suite.

"What are we looking for?" Loretta asked.

"The Telly Award."

Then, the camera exposed the entire suite, showing the desk and the open balcony door the officers were walking in and out of.

Ruth pointed at the desk. "Where's the Telly Award? He always has it on his desk. He says in the other video that he always places it on his desk for motivation."

Loretta shrugged. "Maybe he moved it."

"No, I don't think so. He says it's his pride. Romeo even says that he never goes anywhere without it. But it's not here. It's not on his desk where he had it in the previous videos." Ruth scrolled the video back a little to replay the part where Romeo entered the suite. It was the best visual of the place in the video. She shook her head. "It's not on the shelves or the table."

Loretta huffed. "What does this have to do with his murder?"

"I don't know," Ruth said, still watching the video. "But I have a feeling that this is a clue."

"I think it's sleep deprivation."

"I have to tell Humphrey."

"You'll get in trouble. Besides, you think Humphrey is slow and stupid."

"I don't think he's stupid. That's just mean. I just think he's a little slow witted. But that's why I'm here, to speed up the process and nab the killer."

"No." Loretta crossed her arms. "You're here to make delectable desserts."

Ruth got up, grabbing her purse. "Whatever. I've got to talk to Officer Humphrey."

Loretta shook her head slowly. "I swear, Ruth. You have some crazy addiction to trouble. You know, Humphrey is going to nail you to a wall or lock you in the brig when he finds out what you've been up to."

Loretta's words barely registered as Ruth hastily exited the cafe and hurried to Humphrey's office.

CHAPTER 22

"You did what?!" Humphrey's face looked like a shiny, ripe tomato ready to burst.

Ruth didn't quite understand his over-the-top reaction. Perhaps she'd bothered him too late? His grumpiness certainly seemed to grow worse in the middle of the night. "With all due respect, sir, don't you think you're being a tad bit overdramatic?"

"Overdramatic?" His eyes went wide. Now Ruth knew for sure, he was definitely going to burst. "Let's see, Ruth. You just told me that you hunted down Hector, a VIP guest on the ship and the new executive producer of a mega-hit show, confronted him on the beach where he was lounging, and accused him of *murder!*"

"Well now, when you put it that way, it sounds bad.

But at least we now know that he wasn't the murderer. And may I just add, he was working on a script for the new season. Not lounging on the beach."

Humphrey ran both hands through his graying hair, clearly agitated. "Ruth, I thought I told you to stay away from the cast and crew of *Darkness into Light*. It's like you deliberately disobey me. You know you could lose your job. Aren't you worried about that?"

"Truthfully, sir, I'm more worried about your blood pressure."

"That's it!" Humphrey scoffed. "You leave me no choice. I'm going to have to contact your superior." He picked up the receiver of his phone.

"Romeo's video is up on Friendbook," Ruth blurted out. "It's public."

Humphrey slammed the receiver down. "Huh?"

Ruth took a deep breath. "The night of Jay's murder."

"Shh." Humphrey looked at the door and then back at Ruth. "Don't say the 'm' word. What if someone hears you? We can't chance this getting out."

"Fine," Ruth said. "The night of Jay's mishap."

Humphrey waved his hands at her. "No, don't say 'mishap' either. Still sounds bad. Say, 'incident.'"

Ruth rolled her eyes. "The night of Jay's incident, Romeo was recording. You confronted him that night and asked if he was recording. He said no."

Humphrey narrowed his eyes. "How do you know that?"

"Isn't it obvious? He lied to you. Of course, he was recording, and he posted it on Friendbook."

"Friendbook?" Humphrey rubbed his chin. Ruth knew if he called her superior and outed her, he would also be in trouble for allowing Jay's incident to leak on one of the most popular social media platforms.

He took a long, deep breath, his eyes closed. When he opened them, he turned to Ruth. "You need to let this go, Ruth. Or we will both be in trouble."

"No can do, Chief," she said, grinning.

Humphrey let out a frustrated breath. "Please, Ruth. Tell me you didn't do anything crazy."

"Not yet." It was clear he didn't like the sound of that. "So, in these videos, Jay has his Telly Award."

"His what?"

"Telly Award. You know, the award for best telenovela?"

Humphrey shook his head, clearly lost.

"Doesn't matter. Anyway, he never went anywhere without his Telly Award. He always placed it on his desk."

"That's what this is all about?" Humphrey asked. "A trophy that has gone missing that was probably relocated by Jay himself?" Humphrey waited for a response, but Ruth didn't give him one. Instead, she sat there, staring back at him.

Humphrey scoffed. "You are unbelievable, Ruth. Impossible." He rubbed his head, then opened his desk drawer, pulling out a keycard. He rose and made his way around the desk. "All right, Ruth. Let's go."

"Go where?"

"To Jay's suite. You need proof, and that's what I'm going to give you. I'll prove to you once and for all that this is all nonsense. And then you have to promise me something."

"What?"

"If I take you to his suite to find the Telly Award, probably in a cabinet or stored away somewhere so it wouldn't get dusty or something, you have to stop. No more investigating. No more questioning people. You leave the crew and the actors alone. In fact, all the passengers. If I catch you even talking to a passenger off-duty, I will have you suspended."

Now, Ruth didn't like the sound of *that*. But she stood, keeping her head held high, and she gave Humphrey one sharp nod.

"All right, then," he said. "Let's go."

Ruth grabbed her purse, and they walked to the elevator.

This was her last chance. Hopefully, it would lead them to another clue or something.

When the doors opened on the elevator, Humphrey offered Ruth to get in first, and he followed behind her, slapping the button for deck seventeen. They were both silent as they were elevated to the seventeenth level. When they got out, Ruth noted that the hallway was quiet. They made a right and walked all the way down to almost the end of the hall before arriving to suite number 1707. Humphrey slid the keycard, and as the light on the lock turned green, he swung the door open.

Ruth was now confronted by the huge pink-and-blue painting of a woman that hung on the other side of the foyer, opposite her. The woman's features were delicate and soft as the colors that made up the painting, but something about the monstrous art piece made her feel overwhelmed. It was probably the enormous, intricate brass frame.

Humphrey passed Ruth, waddling across the foyer and around to the right. The suite was even bigger in person. As Ruth was filled with awe at the sight of the place, Humphrey stopped and stared at her. "Hey, if anyone finds out you're in here, we're both in a huge heap of trouble."

Ruth snapped out of her trance. "It's not every day I get to be in a beautiful suite such as this, let alone a crime scene, but I understand. We must get down to business."

"Just don't touch anything," Humphrey said, raising an eyebrow. "The last thing we need are your fingerprints in here."

Ruth gave him a salute. "Right." She made her way around the couch and living area and headed straight for the study, when she stopped abruptly.

Humphrey stopped too. "What? What is it?"

Ruth cocked her head. "The Telly Award. It's on the desk again."

"Huh?" Humphrey walked up to Ruth and stopped next to her. "Okay, so there it is. It's not gone. You were wrong, and we can go now."

"No, I'm not wrong." Ruth eyed the gold figurine with the pointed wings, standing on a black marble platform. "I watched the video a dozen times. It wasn't there."

"Really? A dozen times?" Humphrey asked, apparently skeptical of the number.

"Okay, maybe not that many times, but enough to know with one hundred percent certainty that it was not there." She walked up to the trophy.

"Ruth, don't touch it."

Ruth squinted, studying it closely.

"Don't breathe on it either," Humphrey added.

Ruth ignored him, pulling a clean silk hankie out from her purse. She picked up the trophy and knelt down so that she was eye-level to the desk.

"Ruth," she heard Humphrey grumble.

Ruth stood back up and turned to Humphrey. "Dust."

"Of course, there's dust. No one was in here for days, not even room service."

"Yes, and therefore, there would be a thin layer of dust already accumulating, which it is, leaving no untouched areas." Ruth pointed to the area the trophy was sitting. "Except under the trophy."

"Okay?"

"Sir, there's a layer of dust under the trophy as well. Which means this trophy was placed here very recently." Ruth began eyeballing the Telly Award in her hand.

"I don't know, Ruth. Maybe one of my men moved it for some reason. I'll have to talk to them."

"I don't think it was one of your men." Ruth turned the trophy so Humphrey could see what she was looking at.

Humphrey leaned in to get a better look.

"Now, don't breathe on it," Ruth said, giving Humphrey a stern look. He inched back, and she could tell he was now using only shallow breaths. "What's that?" Ruth asked, pointing to a spot just under the angel's wing.

Humphrey's eyes went wide. "Is that blood?"

Bringing the Telly Award closer to her face, Ruth squinted. Something wasn't quite right. Was it the color? "I don't know," she mumbled. "Maybe not."

"What else could it be?"

Ruth tilted the trophy in her hand ever so slightly, and the red blotch shimmered subtly. "Look at this."

Humphrey leaned in again. "That doesn't seem right."

"It's not blood."

"Well, there goes that evidence."

Ruth clicked her tongue. "Oh, Harry, if only you knew. This is even better." She set the trophy back down on the desk. "I'd suggest you bag this sucker up in one of your evidence baggie things." She put her hankie back into her purse. "And after you do that, we have a lot to discuss."

"A lot to discuss?" Humphrey asked, perplexed. "Oh, Ruth—"

"I have a lot to catch you up on. I say we go back to your office, and I'll fill you in." Ruth headed for the foyer.

"Whoa, whoa, whoa," Humphrey marched up behind her. "Now, you just hold on one second."

Ruth turned around. "Don't you test me. You're already in some deep doo doo with Romeo's video leak, and if you don't want to get into anymore trouble, you'll listen to me."

Humphrey withdrew a step, obviously taken aback by Ruth's assertiveness.

"Besides," Ruth continued, "you help me, and I may just be able to get you out of this."

Humphrey crossed his arms. "Really?"

"Yes, Harry. In fact, I might just make you a hero."

CHAPTER 23

The next day, Ruth and Humphrey headed down the hall to Suite 1705, tailed by her two friends, Loretta and Wanda. Following them were several officers. It was a sea day, and the ship was on its way back to its original port in Florida, ending the trip, though that wouldn't be until tomorrow morning.

When Ruth reached the suite she was looking for, she overheard a woman say, "I'm sorry I have to do this."

"Please, Catalina. Don't. You don't have to do this. We can fix it."

Catalina laughed. "Fix it? We can't fix it. We are way beyond that." There was a moment of silence and Ruth swore she heard a gun cocking. "I'm sorry, Romeo, but everyone already knows. This is the end. I have to kill you now." Ruth's eyes went wide as Humphrey slid the key card through the door slot and flung it open.

Catalina gasped as she held the gun with both hands, pointing it at Romeo. He had his hands up and looked like a deer in headlights.

"Put down the gun!" Humphrey yelled.

The blonde woman looked at all of them in horror. "What?" she said in a thick Spanish accent.

"Put the gun down," Humphrey repeated. He was obviously nervous, as his underarms weren't just damp, they were drenched, and beads of sweat were rolling down his forehead.

Catalina lowered the gun, her elbows now bent. She looked at the gun and then back at the officers. "It isn't real."

Humphrey swallowed hard. "I don't care."

"But it's just a prop. I'll prove it." Catalina tilted the gun to show them. "Look."

"Ma'am, put it down!" Humphrey repeated.

Catalina's eyes went wide. "Okay." She set the gun down gently on the floor next to her feet.

"Now I want you to kick it over to me."

Catalina did as she was told, her hands now up like Romeo's.

"What is going on here?" Romeo demanded as Humphrey picked up the gun with a glove and plopped it into an evidence bag that one of the other officers held.

"We were just about to ask your friend that," Humphrey said, nudging Ruth.

Ruth stepped up in front of everyone.

"Ruth?" Romeo said. "We were just practicing our lines. I don't understand." Then Romeo dropped his arms. "What is this about?" he demanded. Ruth had never seen Romeo look so angry before. She had to admit, it was slightly intimidating.

Ruth held her head up. "This is about Jay Juan."

"Oh?" Catalina said with a relieved chuckle. "I know nothing about that."

"I don't think that's entirely true."

Catalina tilted her head to the side slightly. "What are you getting at?"

"The night Jay Juan died," Ruth said. "You were there."

"What?" Romeo said. He shot a glance at Catalina. "Is that true?"

"It was a hectic night," Catalina said. "Especially with the meet-and-greet."

"What did you do after the meet-and-greet?" Ruth asked.

"I had dinner and then I went to my suite and read over some lines for the show. Then I went to bed."

"You forgot that you got your nails done that night too."

Catalina locked eyes with Ruth. "I suppose I might have. I don't remember. Like I said, it was a hectic day."

"Interesting you would forget something like that when the next morning you needed a touch up."

"So?" Catalina shrugged. "It's not unique to need a touch up."

"It is when you're adamant about getting one done when the salon is booked. See, you made such a fuss about it that the manager of the salon did it herself."

Catalina scoffed. "I didn't—" Wanda stepped in front of the officers, revealing herself to Catalina. The blood in her face drained at the sight of the nail technician. "Well, maybe if the salon would have gotten it right the first time."

Wanda's face flushed. "My girls and I are professionals. We wouldn't have botched up a nail that bad."

Catalina folded her arms in front of her chest. "I really don't see how any of this has to do with Jay Juan's death."

"What color did you get?" Ruth asked Catalina.

"I don't remember what it was called."

"May I see your nails?" Ruth pointed to her hand.

Catalina's brows furrowed. "What?"

"If you have nothing to hide, then there's nothing to worry about," Ruth offered.

"Fine." Catalina thrust her hand out. "Not sure what this will prove, anyway."

Ruth took her hand, eyeing the nails. It was time to release the bulldog that was Wanda. She glanced over her shoulder, still holding Catalina's hand, and called for her. "The sample."

Wanda grinned, pulling out a packet of swatches, and flipped to the marked page. She held the color swatch next to Catalina's nails, and Humphrey stepped over to see. They all looked at each other.

Wanda's brow arched. "Devilishly Divine Cherry," she said.

Just then, Gustavo came out from the bathroom. "What is going on in here?"

"We're about to solve the mystery behind Jay Juan's murder," Ruth said, without breaking eye contact with Catalina.

"How so?" Gustavo asked.

Wanda handed the sample swatch to Humphrey, who took it back to the other officers.

Ruth straightened. "The day you all boarded the ship, Romeo posted a video of everyone in Jay's suite. Romeo, here, also made it a point in the video to show the Telly Award on Jay's desk. Jay responded that he keeps it wherever he is working to keep him motivated. Then Romeo shot another video the night of Jay's murder, in which he walked into the crime scene and was recording the officers walking in and out from the balcony where Jay was apparently thrown over. We already knew there was blunt force trauma to Jay's head that could've happened during his fall, though we weren't sure how at the time, since there was nothing to hinder his fall. Then we realized that someone had locked the balcony door." Ruth shook her head. "Big mistake, because the balcony door could only be locked from the inside."

"But I still don't see what any of this has to do with me," Catalina said. "Or my nails."

"Ah, that's where you come in," Ruth said. "I saw the video of the night the officers were investigating Jay's death, and I noticed that the Telly Award was missing. I didn't notice it at first, but when I did, I had a growing suspicion."

"That's when we found this." Wanda held up the evidence bag with the trophy inside. "Has your DNA all over it."

Loretta nudged Wanda.

Ruth shook her head at her friend's error, but she didn't correct her either. She didn't want to embarrass her in front of everyone.

Catalina chuckled. "My DNA is nowhere on it. Jay wouldn't let anyone touch that thing."

"You're right that your DNA isn't on it," Ruth said, "because you took your time wiping it down, I'm sure. It was missing ever since Jay's death, until someone placed it back on his desk. That someone was you." Ruth took the evidence bag and showed Catalina. "Your nail polish, Devilishly Divine Cherry with a subtle shimmer, is under the wing."

Wanda crossed her arms and smiled smugly. "Guess you missed a spot."

"But why would *I* want to kill Jay Juan?" Catalina said.

"I wondered that too. But then I remembered you said on the set that you couldn't believe you let a big opportunity slip between your fingers. I also remembered in one of the earliest videos, you came out of Jay's office in quite a huff, with a folder in your hand. The tab on that folder read, 'Contract.'"

Catalina's eyes flashed with anger. "You don't understand!" Catalina cried. "I was going nowhere with this show. Maria and Romeo were the true stars. I finally got an opportunity to star in a Hollywood movie..."

"But Jay wouldn't let you."

"He said he owned me for three more years. Three more years! I'd be thirty by that time! And despite what they say about thirties being the new twenties, in the movies, thirties are now your forties, and you know what happens to a woman in her forties in Hollywood? Your career is over. I wasn't about to let this man take my youth and the best opportunity that would make me a real star."

"So, you got angry and you picked up the Telly Award, hitting him as hard as you could over the head."

"I swung it like it was a Louisville slugger baseball bat," she said through her teeth, tears welling up in her eyes.

"But I would assume Jay was a little too heavy for you to throw overboard."

Catalina glanced over at Gustavo, who was still standing off to the left, just outside the room he had come out of. She shifted her gaze back to Ruth and the officers. "Not really. He wasn't as heavy as you think."

Ruth cocked her head to one side, looking her up and down. "He's twice your size, at least."

Just then, Gustavo took off running.

"Oh, come on," Humphrey whined. The man wasn't a runner. His flabby physique made that obvious. The officers next to him took off after the man. Though, Ruth didn't know what any of them were complaining about. He couldn't go far. "You," Humphrey said, pointing at Catalina. "Don't move."

"Don't worry, sir," Wanda said, crossing her arms and planting her feet. She squinted her eyes at Catalina. "I'll keep an eye on her."

Humphrey nodded and followed his men through the back of the suite. It didn't take long for them to catch up to Gustavo and apprehend him. They dragged him back into the room where Catalina, Romeo, Ruth, and her friends were.

Catalina turned to Gustavo. "Don't say anything more. These men aren't even real police officers. They're just officers of the sea. That doesn't mean anything."

Ruth turned to Humphrey, who looked hurt but only for a split second, before he turned to Romeo and asked, "You get it?"

Romeo nodded, holding up his phone. "I captured it all on video."

Catalina whipped herself toward Romeo. "What?"

Romeo smiled, walking the phone over to Humphrey as he held out another evidence bag. Romeo plopped the device into the bag, and Humphrey sealed it, turning to Catalina. "I'm sorry, what were you saying?"

"You!" Catalina squealed in frustration, knowing her fate was now sealed along with the evidence bag that held the phone. She glared at Romeo. "That's why you were so eager to run over our old lines. You weren't worried about growing rusty between season shoots. You set me up!"

Romeo stood by Ruth. "When my friend Ruth and her pals showed me the evidence in my videos last night, it was obvious. How could I work with murderers? How could you hurt Jay? He helped us all be who we are today. You should be ashamed."

"He helped you, not me," Catalina said, her face red with rage. "He was trying to ruin me."

Romeo shook his head. "You were nothing before he gave you the part of Catalina. You just wanted more, and your greediness led to murdering a good man who gave us all a wonderful opportunity." He looked at Humphrey. "Take them away."

"Okay, guys," Humphrey said, puffing out his chest. "Take them to the holding cell. We will be at port soon, where they will be taken into custody for the murder of Jay Juan."

Catalina squirmed as the men holding her escorted her out of the suite. "You can't do this. Let go of me!"

Humphrey walked up to Ruth. "How did you know Gustavo would give himself up like that?"

"Honestly, I didn't." She looked at Humphrey, who dropped his shoulders in surprise. "I only assumed. After I saw them on set together, I realized that they may be more than just friends. The way they looked into each other's eyes, and you know there's a high percentage of actors who play lovers that end up in a romantic relationship. At least, that's what Wanda told me."

Wanda turned around. "It's in those magazines they have in the salon. I can only assume that they are at least somewhat reliable."

Humphrey rolled his eyes. "You're lucky, Ruth."

"No," Ruth said. "*We're* lucky. If it wasn't for us cracking this case, your boss would have your head next to mine on a platter for the video leak."

Humphrey sighed. "You're right."

Loretta walked up to both of them. "Okay, enough with the mush. Let's go to the casino!"

Wanda cheered, but all Ruth could do was groan.

CHAPTER 24

The next morning was port day, when all the passengers would get off the *Splendor of the Seas*, completing another cruise trip. Gerald was saying goodbye to all the passengers as they disembarked.

When Ruth, Loretta, and Wanda approached him, he said, "Well, now, if it isn't Ruth Shores and the gang. Don't tell me you are getting off the ship too."

Ruth regarded him. "Just for a short while. We'd like to take a walk."

"Ah, cabin fever getting to ya?"

"Sure, Gerald. That's exactly what it is."

Gerald gave her a pat on the shoulder as the women exited the ship. "Be sure to be back before 3 p.m. We'll be taking off again for another adventure, and you don't want to miss it."

Ruth turned back to Gerald. "I wouldn't miss it for the world." She gave him a big smile and made her way down the gangway with her friends.

They walked along the path, passing the crowds. It was nice to take in the fresh air before she had to be back in the kitchen and before John had another catastrophe started.

"Can you believe it?" Wanda said. "We nabbed ourselves two murderers. We should be detectives."

"Let's not get ahead of ourselves," Ruth said.

Loretta nodded. "Ruth's right. We all could have been in really big trouble if it weren't for Ruth figuring it out."

Ruth nodded. "But it was still an adventure. And that's what life should be all about. One adventure after another. Otherwise, it would be so boring."

Loretta turned to Ruth. "Don't get any more crazy ideas."

Ruth laughed.

As they continued their stroll, she heard her name being called. It was Romeo. He was jumping up and down and waving at her.

Loretta shielded her eyes from the sun with her hand. "Is that Romeo calling?"

"It sure is," Wanda said. She sounded like a giddy schoolgirl.

When they all waved back, he motioned for them to come over. He was standing with another incredibly gorgeous man, and Ruth was intrigued. She'd never seen this man before. She grabbed her friends, and they headed over to Romeo.

"Hi, friends," he said as they approached. "I want you all to meet Enrique Suave."

"Enrique Suave," Wanda said, holding out her hand to him. "Pleasure to meet you."

Enrique took her hand. "Pleasure is all mine," he said, giving her hand a small peck. Wanda giggled girlishly.

"Enrique is going to take my place in the show," Romeo said, excited. "Well, not exactly take my place. There is only one Romeo, and there will only ever be one Romeo, of course. But he will be the new heartthrob."

"I see," Ruth said. "But I think I speak for all of us when I say that we will miss you in *Darkness into Light*. What will you do now?"

"I guess I can tell you all, since you already know many of our secrets. But this has to stay a secret. Unlike my unfortunate co-worker, my contract was up, and instead of renewing it, I got a serious role in a Hollywood movie, which has always been a dream of mine. So, I'll be starring in a series of Hollywood romances. The first one is called, *A Lover's Journey*."

"Oooh," Loretta said. "Sounds romantic."

He chuckled. "It is."

The familiar clacking of stilettos approached them. Ruth turned to see Maria Melendez with her long, wavy hair bouncing with each confident step. She wore white-rimmed sunglasses and had a cellphone pressed to her ear.

"Maria!" Romeo shouted. "Come meet Enrique!"

She looked up and waved at him, still talking on her phone. Ruth could hear her say, "Absolutely not. Over my dead body!"

Ruth raised an eyebrow and Loretta nudged her. "Don't get any ideas," her friend whispered.

As Maria approached them, she hung up her phone and smiled at Romeo. "Rafael!" She came in and gave him a hug. "How are you doing after all of this? Who'd imagine that the people we worked with every day would do such a horrible thing."

"I'm all right," Romeo said. They both smiled at each other for a moment before Enrique cleared his throat lightly. "Ah, yes," Romeo said. "Maria, I want you to meet Enrique Suave."

Maria furrowed her eyebrows and cocked her head. "Enrique who?"

"Enrique—"

Maria's phone played a salacious Spanish tune. She

put up a slender finger and answered it. "Now what?" She let out a heavy sigh. "What do I even pay you for? Well, you tell him a quarter mil. That's my final offer."

Romeo looked at everyone. "She's always so busy. Busy, busy woman."

Maria hung up the phone. "I apologize." Then she looked at Enrique. "So, you are going to be the next star?"

Enrique blushed. "I could never fill Romeo's shoes, of course. But yes."

"Good for you. Can't wait to work with you." She held out her hand and he took it. She gave him a firm shake and then turned to Ruth.

"Ruth," Maria said. "Just the woman I've been looking for."

"Oh?" Ruth said.

"Listen, Ruth, I just wanted to apologize for how I treated you at the bar the other night."

"That's okay."

"No, it wasn't. I've been so stressed out." Tears began to well up in Maria's soft brown eyes, but she swallowed hard, obviously pushing down the emotions that were boiling up. "I'm going through a divorce."

"Oh, no."

"And my ex is trying to take everything he can from

me, even though I know he's been cheating." Maria sighed.

Now everything was falling into place for Ruth. Maria hadn't been referring to Jay Juan when she made those threats but to her soon-to-be ex-husband. "I'm so sorry to hear that. I accept your apology. And I'm sorry for prying."

Maria nodded as she dabbed her eye, making sure the dampness wasn't ruining her perfect makeup. A limousine pulled up, and she turned to face everyone again. "That's for me," she said, referring to the limo that had just stopped in front of them. "I must go. It was nice to meet you, Enrique. Nice to see you all." She blew them a couple of kisses and hopped in. Cracking the window, she gave one final wave as she was whisked away.

"So, what's going to happen to the show now that Catalina and Gustavo are gone?" Wanda asked.

"Ah, yes," Romeo said. "So, I talked to Hector, and he said he rewrote the script for the next season. In the first episode, they're going to have doubles of Catalina and Gustavo walk into their beautiful new house. The viewers are only going to see them from behind as they walk in and close the door. A few moments later, it'll explode! Like Romeo's final revenge!"

"A twist!" Wanda shouted.

"Shh." Romeo put a finger up to his lips. "My friends, we have to keep this our little secret until it airs next season."

Wanda nodded. "Oh, right."

"I can't wait until the season finale airs," Loretta said.

"You already know what's going to happen," Ruth said.

"I know, but I want to see it rather than just reading it."

"Ah, yes," Romeo said. "That shall be in the next couple weeks. Anyway, I'd like to keep in touch with you all. You are all a part of my Friendbook group?"

Loretta jumped up. "I am!"

"No," Ruth said. "I don't have an account, and I don't wish to have one."

Romeo smiled. "No worries, my friends. I have a great agent. He can track anyone down."

"That's a little worrisome," Ruth said.

Romeo let out a soft chuckle.

A couple of weeks later, Wanda was rounding everyone up into the crew lounge to watch the season finale of *Darkness into Light*. Ruth pretended not to be interested as she sat among her friends, but secretly, she too was excited. After reading the script weeks before, she wanted to see how it played out on screen, especially with the absence of Jay Juan.

She'd even made an extra batch of the caramel cupcakes, only this time, they'd used John's recipe. He had come up with the idea that instead of making a pretzel crumble, they should dip a mini pretzel in creamy chocolate and place it on top. Ruth loved the idea, and it seemed to be a hit among their co-workers. They were devouring them like a pack of coyotes.

Finally, the *Darkness into Light* theme song began to play and all the women, plus John, took their seats.

Midway through the show, Catalina and Gustavo's suspicions of their partners, Romeo and Maria, having a steamy affair were confirmed.

The camera closed in on Catalina's face. "He will pay for this," she said. "Him and his little tramp."

Later, Catalina and Gustavo met. "Gustavo," Catalina said. "You must kill Romeo."

Gustavo took Catalina by the hand. "I can't do that. I can't hurt someone like that."

Catalina scoffed and pulled her hand away. "If you're not man enough to do it, then I will!" She walked out, slamming the door behind her as Gustavo called after her.

Stomping down the path to the sandy beach,

Catalina got out her phone, putting it to her ear. "Yes, I'd like to purchase a gun." She paused, looking around her. "It's for protection." Before the camera zoomed in for another close-up of Catalina's face, a familiar man walked past in white-and-pink flamingo swimming trunks.

All the women in the lounge broke their trance and turned toward John.

"Oh yeah," he said, eyes still glued to the TV. He took another bite of his cupcake and swallowed. "That's why they had me sign that form. Love those shorts."

John had certainly followed the terms of whatever agreement he'd signed—this was the first Ruth had known about him appearing in a shot of the famed telenovela. The gang of women shook their heads at him and turned their attention back to the screen.

After Catalina acquired a revolver, she followed Romeo to his new beach house, where he was about to meet his lover, Maria. Catalina hid in the bushes, waiting.

There were a few gasps in the crew lounge, and Betty said, "Oh no. This can't be happening." She turned to the other women.

Bertie shook her head. "He'll get out of this. He always does," she said, hopeful.

On-screen, Romeo was looking at the stars, then he

closed his eyes, taking in the salty sea air. "What a beautiful night," he said.

A shadow came up from behind.

The women in the lounge all begun to murmur.

"No," one said as the camera zoomed in on a revolver reflecting the moonlight.

"Romeo, look behind you!" another woman said.

Bang!

The screen went to black and the credits appeared. There was a moment of silence in the lounge as all the women were wide-eyed with shock.

Bertie scoffed. "He can't be dead. They wouldn't do that. They'd lose all their fans."

"I don't know," Betty said. "The gun was aimed at close range. It's not like the person could have missed. That was a shot to kill."

"It's a telenovela," Bertie argued. "Characters have escaped worse and come out alive."

"Maybe," Betty said. "But I wonder how they are going to get around Catalina and Gustavo. I'm assuming they won't be on the show anymore, since they're being accused of Jay's death. It's all over the news."

Betty was right. It was big news, and you couldn't flip on the TV or open a newspaper or magazine without seeing something about it. Everyone from talk shows to late-night shows were asking the same question as Betty.

"I guess we'll have to see when they air the first episode next season," Wanda said.

Betty put her hands on either side of her face. "Oh, I don't think I can wait that long."

"I hope it's not something stupid like going on with the show as if none of this ever happened, or as if these characters never existed," Bertie said. "I'll be so mad."

"Bertie, you're always mad," Wanda said.

Bertie gave her a scowl and grumbled.

"I guess no one will know until they air it," Ruth said.

"Yeah, I'm sure the producers and writers probably don't even know yet. They're probably all scrambling to figure it out as we speak," Loretta said with a wink.

Ruth, Loretta, and Wanda exchanged amused glances and smiled at each other. Ruth had an inkling that Wanda would make sure that everyone was rounded up again to watch the first episode when the season premiere started, and they couldn't wait to see everyone's faces when Catalina and Gustavo were no longer a threat—and Romeo, as if he had come back from the dead, gave his viewers one final, explosive surprise.

# # #

Thank you for reading! Want to help out?

Reviews are a big help for independent authors like me, so if you liked my book, **please consider leaving a review today**.

Thank you!

-Mel McCoy

ALSO BY MEL MCCOY

- Whodunit Pet Cozy Mystery Series -

(Features Ruth's family in Cascade Cove, Florida)

Panic at the Pier

Betrayal at the B&B

Fear at the Ferris Wheel

The Murder Before Christmas

Terror at the Tiki Bar

ABOUT THE AUTHOR

Mel McCoy has had a lifelong love of mysteries of all kinds. Reading everything from Nancy Drew to the Miss Marple series and obsessed with shows like *Murder, She Wrote*, her love of the genre has never wavered.

Now she is hoping to spread her love of mysteries through her new Whodunit Pet Cozy Mystery Series. Centered around a cozy beachside town, the series features a cast of interesting characters and their pets, along with antiques, crafts such as knitting, and plenty of culinary delights.

Mel lives with her two dogs, a rambunctious and bossy Yorkie named Peanut, and a dopey, lazy hound (who snores a lot!) named Murph.

For more info on Mel McCoy's cozy mystery series, please visit: www.melmccoybooks.com

Connect with Mel:

Facebook: facebook.com/CozyMysteryMel
Twitter: twitter.com/CozyMysteryMel

Made in the USA
Middletown, DE
28 October 2020